TAYLOR & MACK - A MAFIA ROMANCE

TRACIE PODGER

Jeanette
Thank you
for all your
Support
Tracie x

Lovely Ju

thank you

for all Support

racist :)

Taylor & Mack

A Mafia Romance

This novella accompanies the Fallen Angel Series but is read as a standalone.

If you would like a free copy of my novella, Evelyn, which also accompanies the Fallen Angel Series, sign to my mailing list here…

http://eepurl.com/clbNTP

Chapter 1

I'd been sent to my bedroom, not as a form of punishment, but to keep me out of the way. Daddy had an important meeting, I'd been told. Of course, telling me to do something and expecting me to actually do it had me chuckling.

I crouched at the top of the vast, pretentiously ornate oak and gold-plated sweeping staircase of our Texas home. I was just out of view, I hoped, from the visitors the maid had opened the door to. An older gentleman walked in. He looked foreign and spoke with an accent I hadn't heard before. Behind him, was the most gorgeous man I'd ever seen. Tall with broad shoulders, muscular arms and fair hair, he stood like a bodyguard protecting his 'boss.' Perhaps I'd made a sound, or shuffled a little, but he'd been alerted to my presence. He glanced up the stairs and his gaze came to rest on me. I straightened, knowing Daddy would be mighty cross, but not caring. I wanted the man to see me. I gave him a coy smile and a little flick of my hair as I'd seen

Momma do many times. I doubted he could see the batting of my long eyelashes but I gave it a try anyway. He smiled a little before his attention was drawn toward my daddy. I sighed; annoyed the moment had been broken.

I craned my neck to watch him walk toward Daddy's home office, and then scowled at the maid as she looked up at me and smirked. I didn't like her one bit, I was sure Daddy was fucking her and I wanted to catch them at it. Momma tolerated Daddy's 'indiscretions,' as long as he didn't bring them home. The maid, and I didn't know her name nor care to, was a little too close to home.

I gave it a few more minutes before I descended the stairs and found Momma in the kitchen, she was directing the maid, and by the tone of her voice, was displeased with her. I gave her a good 'ol Southern smile as I passed.

"Momma, who are the men with Daddy?" I asked.

"Just some business associates, Taylor, nothing for you to worry about," she replied, fixing her lipstick as she spoke.

My momma was always perfectly made-up. I couldn't recall a time I'd seen her without makeup or less than perfect hair. She smiled to herself in her small silver compact mirror before clicking it closed and placing it in the cosmetic bag on the kitchen counter.

"The older man was foreign, wasn't he?" I asked.

"Italian, I believe. Although he lives in D.C. now."

"What about the other one, the blond guy?"

Momma glanced sideways at me. Her brow furrowed a little as if silently questioning why I wanted to know. I felt my cheeks color and then watched her eyebrows rise in surprise.

"Taylor, you stay out of your daddy's business, you understand me?"

I nodded, chastised, but knowing I wouldn't stay out of Daddy's business. There was something that had intrigued me about the blond man. It had been hard to determine his age, although it was clear he was certainly older than I was.

"Let me fix your hair," she said, turning me by my shoulders.

She untied the braid and ran her fingers through my blonde hair. "You have such pretty hair," she said, tying it expertly.

The maid laid a tray with some tea for Momma beside us, that time she didn't attempt to catch my attention but kept her eyes lowered. Momma didn't thank her and she scuttled away.

"She needs to go," I said.

"She does, and she will. But finding the right staff is so hard nowadays," Momma replied.

"Get a man, Daddy might not be so *friendly* then."

Momma laughed as she turned me to face her.

"You see too much, my darling. However, that's not such a bad idea."

At eighteen, I was old enough to know the *signs*. Although still a *virgin* (I'd made out plenty of times), I'd had to fight off many a *schoolboy,* who thought he was man enough to take my virginity. Of course, Daddy would have shot any boyfriend I was caught with, so he'd regularly tell me.

"How about a little shopping?" Momma said.

Shopping and spending time with my momma, were my two favorite things. I nodded enthusiastically. I wasn't spoiled, not like some of my friends, although I did come from wealth and privilege. I wasn't entirely sure what my father did for work. He'd brush away my questions, telling me to concentrate on my schooling and looking beautiful. He was an old-fashioned man at heart, not wanting his wife to work, and being his only child, he doted on me.

"Good morning, Miss Taylor," I heard as I left the house.

Carl had a car idling outside and was standing beside the open rear door. I knew that his *partner in crime*, as I called him, Rick, would be sitting in the driver's seat already. Momma and I never went anywhere without Carl shadowing us. I loved him, but hated the lack of freedom and envied my friends that had it. On the odd occasion I was allowed to the movie theater, or out for a meal, Carl was always there.

Momma walked down the steps from the front door, and as always, Carl leapt forward to take her hand and help her down the last few. Not that she needed the help, but she smiled her thanks before ushering me into the back of the car. She gracefully slid in beside me.

The car, a black Lincoln Town Car, had dark windows and was bulletproof according to Rick. I wasn't sure if that was meant to be a joke or not. It was hot and stuffy and I asked him to crank up the air-conditioning. Momma reached over to take my hand; she gave me a beautiful smile before turning to look out the window.

It was the last smile she'd ever give, and although it took me a long time to come to terms with that, I was thankful for it.

At first I wasn't sure what I was seeing yet, in hindsight, it was so obvious. Rick had raised a handgun and without hesitation had shot Carl through the side of the head. I didn't think Momma and I even had time to scream before that gun was leveled at us. He held it over his shoulder looking at us in the rearview mirror. Although I could only see his eyes, the wrinkles to the side of them suggested he was smiling. What he had to smile about, I wasn't sure.

"Get down on the floor, Taylor," Momma said, not looking at me. I sat frozen, unable to send the signal from my brain to my limbs.

It wasn't the sound I'd normally hear from a handgun but more of a loud puff. I stared at my momma, at the streak of red that ran down the side of her beautiful face. It was a red that matched the color of her lips; her mouth opened and closed, yet produced no sound. I threw myself to the floor behind the driver's seat, not sure if I was protected or not. It surprised me to learn I hadn't made a sound. Not one sob, not one scream, nothing. I searched for Momma's handbag and with shaking hands, reached in to find her gun. The tears started to fall when I couldn't find it. And then I prayed.

I felt Rick grab my hair and pull me slightly upward. He still held one hand on the steering wheel, and I wondered what he'd done with the gun. I screamed at that point. I dug my nails into his hand and scraped as hard as I could. I bashed myself against his seat back, hoping to dislodge him a little. I then remembered something I'd either seen in a movie or been told to do. I braced my feet against his seat and pushed backward. I heard the rip as a handful of hair was pulled from my scalp. I pushed and pushed until I was back on the seat, and he'd had no choice but to let go. I threw myself over my momma, burrowing underneath her while trying to open the car door. Rick had sped up and I knew the doors wouldn't open until he unlocked them, but I hoped for a miracle.

How the thought that I needed someone to see my distress came to me, I wasn't sure. Although the road we traveled along wasn't particularly busy, there was oncoming traffic. I found a strength I didn't believe I had when I pushed Momma forward and between the front seats. Rick startled and the car swerved. I heard the honk of a horn and silently begged whoever had done that had also seen Momma and her bloodied face.

Ahead of us were stoplights, yet Rick made no attempt to slow the car. The intersection was busy and whether what I did was reckless or not, I climbed over Momma and grabbed the steering wheel. Rick punched my arms, he swung to reach my head, but as he did, I wrenched the wheel to the left. I didn't remember much more, other than hearing the squeal of metal, the crunch as the car crumpled into an oncoming truck, and then silence other than the horn giving a continuous blast.

The smell roused me. It was an electrical type of smell mixed with burning rubber. I also heard a groan and it took a moment to realize the sound had come from me. I hurt all over, my body ached, and I cried out as I tried to move myself onto the back seat. I could see Rick bent slightly forward and panic welled up inside me. A fist bashing on the window startled me. I looked to see a man trying to punch through the side window. I shouted for help, all thoughts of my aching body abandoned. I kicked at the door but it was too buckled and, I guessed, still locked. A blast of air had me spinning toward the driver's seat. Someone had opened the door and disengaged the locks. I scrambled over an unconscious Rick, exiting the car, falling to my knees.

"He killed my momma," I heard myself say over and over.

I'd never before welcomed the sound of sirens but in that moment, I thanked the Lord for them. Then I heard a voice that metaphorically brought me to my knees. My daddy was calling me. I saw him run along the road, weaving in and out of cars. Behind him were two of his guys and the blond man I'd seen at home. I think I finally passed out at that point.

Chapter 2

I woke in a hospital bed with Daddy sitting beside me. He held his head in his hands but when he heard me shuffle up the bed, he looked up. The sight of his red-rimmed eyes and his sallow complexion threw me. That was, until I remembered. He leapt from his chair and cradled me in his arms as I sobbed.

"Hush now, baby. You're okay," he whispered.

"Momma..." was all I managed in reply.

The sound of my daddy's tears broke me further. We sat for God knows how long, holding each other and crying. Not once did I ask the question that was burning a hole in my mind—Why?

Arriving home, just a few days later, was the hardest thing I'd ever had to do. Everywhere I looked it reminded me of my momma. I thought I'd even heard her soft voice on many occasions, as I wandered from room to room, not knowing what to do with myself. Daddy tried to get me to talk about what had happened, but it was just too hard. I told him, and the police, what had physically happened, but I closed my mind off to the images that fought to be seen, especially at night.

Daddy became angry, not with me, but with his *investigation team*. Many times I heard him shouting behind the closed door of his home office. I watched men leave his office and scuttle off, not one gave me even a cursory glance.

Momma's funeral was a lavish affair and I went through the day on autopilot. Many people attended, including the Italian and the blond guy, whose name I learned was Mack. He made a point to seek me out after the burial.

"How are you doing? Or is that a really dumb question?" he asked, as I stood in one corner of our living room trying to hide.

I shrugged my shoulders. "I guess I'm numb right now," I replied.

"I can imagine. I didn't know your mother but everyone here speaks very highly of her."

"She was loved by many. I just don't understand why Rick…" I couldn't bring myself to finish my sentence.

Perhaps Mack could see my increasing level of distress. When he asked if I'd like to take a walk and get some fresh air, I nodded, already feeling the room closing in on me, and the claustrophobia causing my lungs to constrict.

Despite the heat, a shiver ran over me. I pulled my cardigan around me tightly.

"Why were you there, that day?" I asked, the question only then coming to mind.

"We were doing business with your father," Mack answered.

"No, why did you arrive at the…at the car. I saw you."

"Your father took a call, I guessed from someone at the scene? I happened to have been in a car with the engine running. I drove him there."

"How well do you know my daddy?" We walked down the pathway toward a lawn area where seating was arranged under the trees.

"Not very well. My…friend…knows him well, though. They often do business."

I took a seat on a bench and stared straight ahead, back toward the house. He sat a respectable distance away.

"Taylor, I'm not sure what words to use to express my sorrow for your loss. I can see the pain in your eyes, and I wish I could do something to help you."

His words were spoken so softly, they contradicted his features.

His nose was broken and I wondered if he boxed professionally. He had that look about him. There was an aura of strength around him. He was a protector of people, I imagined.

"Thank you. I just don't know what I'm going to do without Momma." I turned in my seat to face him.

"Why, Mack? Why did Rick shoot Carl and my momma, then try to shoot me? I was absolutely sure he was going to shoot me and I don't know why."

Mack shrugged his shoulders. "I can't answer that, but I wonder if you *were* the target. He could have easily shot you, Taylor, he didn't. There was a reason you survived."

I hadn't thought along those lines at all. As far as I was concerned, he was going to kill me as he had my momma.

I could see Daddy standing on the patio with another man, both were looking toward where we sat.

"I think we've been out of sight for too long. How about we head back into the house?" Mack said.

"I don't want to go back into the house."

"I think your father might appreciate you being there, where he can see you," he said gently.

I sighed and stood. Mack walked beside me, towering above me, as we made our way back to the house.

When I thought it was acceptable, I snuck upstairs to my

bedroom. I threw off the black dress and pulled on some jeans and a t-shirt. I sat on the chair facing the large picture window and looked out at nothing. I wanted to fill my mind with images to dilute the ones that had taken prominence, but it was hard. Instead, I closed my eyes and pictured Mack. His kind words, the soft voice that contradicted his bulk, filled my mind and settled me somewhat. That was until I thought on his words.

There was a reason you survived.

I shuddered at the thought that Rick's intention could have been to kidnap me. That scenario had been something Daddy had warned me about many times. I carried a can of Mace and a rape alarm in my purse. I hadn't taken my purse that day because I thought I was safe with Momma. I thought I was safe with Carl and Rick.

I cried a lot, mostly when I was on my own. I was extremely lonely, banned from leaving the house and left with only my memories and a broken heart for company. Daddy didn't even make dinnertime with me anymore. I sat alone at a vast, polished oak table and was served my meals in silence. The maid, whose name I learned was Monique, became my only companion. As much as I tried to catch her and Daddy together, I never did. I began to wonder if that had been a figment of my imagination.

"Do you want company?" Monique asked, as she laid a plate in front of me.

"That would be nice. When do you eat?" I asked, ashamed I had no idea of her schedule.

"Later, normally."

"Bring your meal and join me," I said.

She gave me a smile and left the dining room, only to return a few minutes later with a sandwich.

"Is that all you're having?" I asked.

"I eat my main meal when I'm at home, with my son."

I stared at her; she didn't appear to be much older than I was.

"Your son?"

"Yes. Jacob is nearly two. I know, I was a very young mom." She chuckled as she spoke.

"Who looks after your son while you're here?"

"His father. We work opposite shifts. It's not easy sometimes, and I miss him, especially all those *firsts*. I missed his first steps and his first words, that was hard. But don't get me wrong, I love my job," she hastily added.

"Did you ever…?" I shook my head; I didn't need to know.

"Your father? No. And I don't think that's a conversation we really need to have right now. I know what you thought, and I couldn't blame you for that. I have eyes, I see what goes on, but I wouldn't ever go there."

"But did he try?"

She didn't reply, and that was all the answer I needed. We ate for a while in silence, and although we didn't speak, I enjoyed having someone sit with me.

"How is the investigation going?" she asked, as she pushed her plate to one side.

"I don't know, I don't get told much. I was interviewed by the police and told that I'd probably need to speak with them again, but that was it really. Daddy seems to be the one in charge and I'm not sure why. It appears that I know very little about him."

Sadness washed over me at the thought.

Later that night, as I lay in bed, I thought on the conversation I'd had with Monique. I was ashamed to realize I didn't know how long she'd worked at the house, and to not know that she had a son seemed significant. I wondered if Momma had known. Maybe I'd been too harsh on her. It wasn't that I was a spoiled brat; Momma wouldn't have had that. I guessed I viewed most females as a threat to Momma's happiness. I'd witnessed her, just the once, shed tears when she'd been confronted with one of Daddy's *indiscretions* at the tennis club. I'd wanted to rip the hair from the woman's head but Momma was always so dignified. Not once would she allow anyone to see they had affected her, normally. I needed to find that strength and dignity myself. Daddy always said I was a hothead, a lot like him.

The days rolled into weeks, the weeks into months and the urge to want to know why my momma had been shot got stronger. With that, I found an ally in Monique. Daddy was out one day, another meeting with men that had me on edge. Men, whose images suggested Daddy wasn't as legitimate as I'd believed.

I stood outside his office door, my hand rested on the doorknob, and I took in a deep breath. I'd rarely ventured into his office, and certainly never when he'd been away. I was about to turn the knob and open the door, when I heard the clip-clop of shoes on the tiled hallway floor.

"Hi, Taylor," I heard Monique say. I spun around to face her.

"Oh, hi. Sorry, I didn't realize you were here," I said, realizing how dumb that sounded considering Monique was in the house every day.

"Are you okay?" she asked.

"Yes. I'm just…getting something from Daddy's office."

"Okay, well if you need help, shout for me," she said then left with a smile.

My heartbeat increased as I opened the door. I wasn't sure what I was anxious about; it was just an office. The room was large with an ornate, dark oak desk that dominated it. Floor-to-ceiling windows gave the room, which reminded me of the Oval Office, lots of light. To one side was a brown leather sofa with a small coffee table in front. I'd sat on the sofa, yet I felt like I was intruding that day. I walked to the large cabinet against the opposite wall and looked at pictures of Momma and me, lifted the stoppers from decanters, and sniffed the contents. I wrinkled my nose at the smell of Daddy's favorite whiskey. At first, I stood in front of Daddy's desk, letting my fingertips brush against the polished wood. Daddy was always so neat. There was a computer to one side and a small stack of papers in the center. I walked around the desk and gently pulled out the chair. I sat, feeling terribly small in the large leather seat.

I wasn't sure what I was looking for; I just wanted to see if there was anything regarding Momma. I flicked through the papers, trying hard not to shuffle the pages in any way. Some of the pages were copies of letters, one looked to be an inventory of sorts. I recognized one or two items on the list. Guns. Daddy had a list of guns sitting on his desk. One page caught my eye. It wasn't written in English but seemed to be some form of Arabic. Underneath, someone had handwritten a translation. My eyes grew wide as I read. Daddy was most certainly selling some of those guns to whoever had written that letter.

Being Texan, having guns, selling guns, wasn't a big deal. But the quantities that appeared to be listed on the letter had me frown. I'd been to the gun store many times, yet this letter seemed to be an order for hundreds of different brands.

I turned on the computer and sighed at the prompt to input a password. I wasn't confident enough to try a few obvious ones and not get caught. Instead I picked up a document I'd found. I flicked through and soon realized Daddy wasn't selling the type of gun I'd handled or seen for sale in the gun store. These were military weapons and I couldn't find one picture that didn't show the weapon being held, or demonstrated, by someone in uniform.

I wasn't sure if there was a connection between what Daddy appeared to do for work and the murder of my mother. I felt foolish at my discovery. I guess, deep down, I knew whatever it was Daddy did was high-risk. I remembered the kidnapping training, all the things I shouldn't have expected to have to know as a teenager. We even had a safe room in the basement of the house. I'd had gun training, despite not wanting to handle a gun. I didn't own one, of course, and I regretted that. Would I have been able to save Momma had I carried a gun? I doubted it, but I was going to talk to Daddy about whether I was old enough.

Chapter 3

I was woken by a noise downstairs. Voices floated up and I was shocked to learn I'd slept in late. For the past few months I'd gotten little sleep, waking frequently from the nightmares that plagued me. I climbed from the bed and piled my hair on top of my head, tying it in a messy bun. I threw on a summer dress and, barefoot, made my way to the landing. As I looked over the bannister, I caught Mack looking up toward me. He gave me a ghost of a smile as my father greeted his friend, the Italian.

I walked down the stairs.

"Good morning," Daddy said as I approached. It was the most he'd spoken to me in months. I smiled at him.

"Morning, Daddy, I overslept today," I replied. I clutched my stomach as it grumbled in protest at not eating breakfast at my regular time.

"Maybe your daughter needs to eat," the Italian man said. I smiled over to him.

He reached out his hand and took one of mine. "Guiseppi. We've briefly met before. You need to eat. I'm always reminding my daughter that she has to eat," he said, with a heavy accent.

Mack didn't introduce himself, he had no need to of course, but I got the impression that it wouldn't have been the thing to do. He stood slightly behind Guiseppi and his stance, his distance, reminded me of Carl when he accompanied Momma or me on our trips. I guessed he was Guiseppi's security.

"I am hungry. I'll leave you to your meeting now. It was nice to see you both again," I said, making a point of looking at Mack.

I caught Daddy look between Mack and me, but he didn't say another word as he ushered his guests to his home office.

"Mmm, he's rather nice," I heard whispered behind me. I turned to see Monique carrying a pile of freshly laundered linens.

I raised my eyebrows at her, but smiled, it was probably the first smile I'd managed in months.

"Perhaps you'd like to know, the guests might be staying over tonight. Hence the bed change," she said, raising the pile of linens in her arms.

"Now, Monique, just why would I be interested in knowing that?" I said, accentuating my accent.

She chuckled as she passed me and headed upstairs. I smiled as I walked toward the kitchen.

"Miss Taylor, what can I get you?" Carol asked.

Carol had been our housekeeper since before I was born, and I loved her as if she were family. She was as old as the hills, as Momma would say, and always had been. I was sure she would still be able to chase me around the house for a chastising, as she had many times when I was a child.

"Just some fruit, I think. Thank you."

"You need a little more than fruit, young lady. You're getting too thin," she said, pursing her lips and placing her hands on her hips. That stance bore no argument.

I laughed, surprising myself at the sound. She smiled as if it was the most delightful sound in the world.

Within a half hour she had bacon, eggs, and fruit laid out on the kitchen island for me. I ate it all, not realizing just how hungry I was. As I was wiping my mouth with a napkin, Mack walked into the kitchen. I wondered if I should have been irked that he seemed to know his way around my house, or that he thought it okay to even do that.

"I'm sorry, your father was calling for...Monique, is it? He wants some coffee so I guess I'm being the errand boy, for now," he said.

"Oh, Monique is changing beds. I saw her go upstairs with linens, she probably didn't hear him," I said, wondering why Daddy didn't just pop his head out the office door and ask me instead.

"I'll get on with that right now," Carol answered.

Instead of heading back to the office, Mack stood and waited. I gestured to a seat beside me, he may as well sit while he waited.

"How are you doing?" he asked.

"Okay, I think. Well, I don't think if I can help it. I mean, I think, especially on what you said when you last visited, and I wished you hadn't said what you did, so I didn't need to think…" I closed my mouth to stop the ramble. Mack unsettled me but not in a horrible way.

Mack laughed and I found myself laughing along with him.

"I *think* I know what you mean," he said.

"Do you get any time off?"

"Time off?"

"I mean, do you have to sit in the meeting, or whatever you have going on in Daddy's office?"

"No. I'm not needed in that office. I just help Joe get where he needs to be, safely."

"So, you're his security?"

"Sort of, I guess. I'm also one his fighters."

I stared at him. I'd guessed that he might have fought.

"Legally, I hope," I said, cocking my head to one side. He didn't answer but gave me a smirk, or a half-smile, which melted me from the inside out.

He shrugged his shoulders.

"Do you win all your fights?"

"Sure do. Although, I don't think I'll do it for much longer, I'm getting too old," he said with a laugh.

"How old are you?" I didn't think he was that much older than me.

"Twenty-five now."

Wow, he was seven years older than I was. I would never have put the difference at that much. My stomach lurched a little and I wasn't entirely sure why. I suspected it was disappointment.

"Coffee's ready," Carol interrupted.

"Thank you. It was good to chat with you, Taylor," Mack said, as he took the tray and headed back to the office.

"Miss Taylor, that man is a little too old for you," Carol said with a chuckle. I felt my cheeks color.

"Seven years isn't a big difference and I really don't know what you mean," I replied, feigning indignation.

She chuckled some more. "He's sure a handsome man, I'll give you that."

"Don't you have something to do?" I asked, straightening in my chair.

"I do, teasing you is one of them," she replied, patting my cheek as she did.

I shook my head but smiled. Not much got past Carol.

"Still, it's nice to hear you laugh, finally," she added.

It had been six, or was it seven, months since that fateful day and I was still to process it completely. I knew everyone had been concerned that I seemed to have withdrawn into myself and not expressed my anger or sadness as much as was expected. However, I had no one to express that to. Carol was the closest person I had, since Daddy had withdrawn so much, but I still didn't feel I could weep on her shoulder and ask for an embrace. I hadn't been able to feel anyone's arms around my shoulders since. All I wanted was for my momma to hold me.

Although Daddy seemed to have kept me on house lockdown the past six months or so, I was at least allowed into the backyard. I decided to take a stroll. I should have been starting college, and I wondered why Daddy seemed to have put a hold on that. I wanted to get involved in fashion design. I had notebooks full of amateurish sketches but it was something I was passionate about.

So was Momma. She'd pour over my designs, giving constructive feedback and helping me to tweak them. We'd agreed that one day, we'd create a room where we could make one of my designs. A wave of sadness washed over me at the thought of all the things we'd planned to do.

My thoughts were interrupted by a shout from the back of the house. I heard Daddy call my name and it surprised me. His tone of voice seemed anxious. I stood from the bench, partly hidden behind a row of trees, and started to make my way back. I was about to raise my hand and give him a wave when I saw commotion behind him. Men started running from the house and Daddy was pushed back inside. At first I froze, fear paralyzing me. Then instinct kicked in and I darted back behind the trees, knowing they wouldn't conceal me completely. To my left was a small pathway that led to a play area I'd had as a child. In that play area, and although not suitable enough to hide in, was a small wooden child's house. I didn't look back until I reached, and hid behind, it.

I crouched down, resting my forehead on my arms that I'd wrapped around my knees. I tried to regulate my breathing by taking in deep breaths. My whole body started to shake as memories of Momma flooded my mind.

What the fuck is going on? I thought.

I'd had a wonderful life until half a year ago. Sure, I had security, it just seemed to be something I'd grown up with and not taken seriously. I'd often wondered if it was just a *status* thing for Daddy. Now, I wasn't so sure.

"Taylor?" I heard. I looked up but stayed where I was.

"Taylor, it's Mack. Where are you?"

I popped my head around the corner of the wooden house. Mack stood scanning the wooded area beyond. I stood.

"What the fuck is going on?" I voiced my thought.

"Nothing, just some people doing something fucking stupid out by the gates."

"Didn't look like *something stupid* to me. Who were those people that ran from the house?"

Mack sighed. "Extra security. I think it's a deal gone bad that your father is involved in. Trust me, Taylor, all I want to do is make sure you're safe and then get Joe home."

"Mack, I'm scared," I said quietly. "I don't want to go back to the house. I want to get as far away from here as possible."

Mack took a step toward me, and although he hesitated initially, he wrapped his arms around me. I sunk into his chest and I felt the most safe I'd been in a while. I couldn't remember a time I'd felt as protected. A deep-rooted loneliness settled inside me when he eventually stepped back.

"Let's get you back to the house, I'm sure your dad is getting worried."

"Why does Daddy need extra security?" I asked, wanting answers before I returned to the house.

"Like I said, I don't know."

"Why are you and Joe here?"

"Joe has business with your father…"

"Guns? I know what my father does, Mack. I'm not stupid."

"No, not guns. Property, Taylor. Joe is into property, lots of it, and your father wants to buy some."

I scanned his face to see if he was lying to me. His features were completely neutral and it threw me. He was too hard to read. I wanted to believe him, but I didn't. That saddened me, yet it didn't quell the attraction I was beginning to feel. Perhaps it was because I felt vulnerable at that time, I hoped so, and yet I hoped not. The developing closeness I felt towards Mack confused me.

I had been lied to my whole life, and I guessed that was for good reason. If Daddy was involved in some shady deals, as the media had insinuated when they'd reported on Momma's death, I imagined he'd shield us from that. To do that, he'd have to lie. Are all lies wrong? I didn't think so. But if Mack lied to me, I think it would hurt more than Daddy just trying to protect me, unsuccessfully it would seem, from his business.

I straightened my back and raised my chin. "Okay, let's go and find out what that was all about," I said, and then strode away, leaving Mack trailing in my wake.

Daddy was sitting in his office with Joe and another guy I didn't recognize, when I barreled through his door. I watched Daddy slowly lift his head from his hands; his face was ashen. He looked worse than he had when Momma died.

"Daddy, what's going on?" I asked.

He didn't answer me for a while but I stood my ground. I wasn't leaving his office without an explanation.

The man I then knew preferred to be called Joe, turned slightly in his seat. "Sit, Taylor. Sit with us," he said.

I wondered why, all of a sudden, he seemed to be in command. Daddy, a normally impressive man, seemed to have shrunk in his presence. I took a seat beside him.

"Your father has gotten himself involved in a deal that…how should I say this? Has caused him some trouble," he said.

"What kind of trouble?" I asked.

"Enough trouble that I have advised him you should move from his house for your safety."

His rather blunt comment stunned me. I looked toward my father with a frown on my brow. Daddy looked everywhere except back at me.

"I'm not leaving my home," I said.

"You have to," Daddy finally spoke.

"Why? What is this all about?" I asked, my voice rose in line with the panic inside me.

"Some people are unhappy with your father, and I believe they'll do whatever is necessary to display that unhappiness," Joe said.

"As in, kill my mother?"

I didn't expect him to nod his head and I felt my heart stop in my chest.

"Daddy, this isn't true. Tell me it's all lies."

Again, my father found the grain of his wooden desk more interesting than answering my question, or even looking at me.

"I've asked Joe to help me. He suggested you go with Mack because no one will know who Mack is," Daddy said.

At that point Mack walked, as if on cue, into the room. Was that the reason he'd been so nice to me? Had he known he was to be my *protector*?

"No. I'm not going anywhere," I said.

"Go pack a case, Taylor, there is no argument on this," Daddy replied.

Mack walked forward and gently leaned down to take my arm, I wrenched it away from him.

"I don't understand. Momma was killed and you've barely spoken to me since. If I was in danger, wouldn't I have been since that day?"

Joe's stare, with his softened features and dark brown eyes, could have been interpreted as pity but I wasn't sure he was that capable of emotion.

"Go, Taylor. Now!" The harshness of Daddy's voice startled me.

"But…"

'Now!" he shouted.

I jumped from my chair and ran to my room. I sat on the edge of my bed in a state of confusion and bewilderment. I wasn't sure how long I'd sat for, but I heard a gentle knock on the door. It opened before I had a chance to invite the intruder in. Mack strode into the room and sat beside me. He sighed.

"Am I in danger?" I asked, my voice quiet.

"I think so. And I'd like to take you away from here, Taylor."

"Why you?"

"Because, as your daddy said, his *friends* don't know me. But they sure as hell would know who Joe is and if you're in his protection, we can keep you safe."

"Who the fuck is Joe then?" I rarely cursed, but I was beyond minding my manners.

"An important man, Taylor. One not to be crossed. You'll be safe with us."

"I don't get a choice in this, do I?"

He gently shook his head.

"How many things am I allowed to bring?" I asked, looking around my room.

"Whatever you want, that'll fit into one case, of course."

I stood and pulled a small case from the shelf in my closet. I filled it with jeans, t-shirts, underwear, toiletries, and a couple of sketchpads. I threw in some sneakers, not bothering with any heeled shoes. The last thing I added was a framed photograph of Momma, and then I zipped the lid closed.

"How long am I going to be gone for?" I asked. I hadn't packed for all the seasons.

"I don't know just yet, but if you're missing anything, we can purchase it."

Mack stood and reached out to take the case from me. I let him, although I'd rather have carried it myself. It seemed that one last act of independence was being erased. I followed Mack down the stairs; standing at the bottom was Joe and my father. We stood and faced each other, awkwardly. I wasn't sure I wanted to step into his nonexistent embrace. Instead he held his hand out to offer me a brown envelope full of money.

"Take this, Taylor. I'll get in touch when I can. Please, believe one thing. I'm doing this, not because I want to, but because I have to. I can't keep you safe, but Joe can."

I took the brown envelope but I didn't utter a word. I was afraid of the cry that would leave my lips had I opened them. I turned and walked away.

I never saw my Daddy again.

Chapter 4

I joined Joe in the back of a very plush vehicle and we drove to the airport. He was heading back to Washington, D.C., he told me. I'd never visited D.C. but I couldn't muster any form of excitement at seeing my nation's capital. I'd stared out the side window for ages after we'd pulled away from my home, praying that it wouldn't be long before I'd be back. I willed the tears that had formed in my eyes not to fall. I was, effectively, in the car with strangers.

"I know this is hard for you, Taylor, but hopefully it won't be for long," Joe said.

His accent was soft and I found myself smiling at him. I always believed I was a good judge of character and there was something about Joe that had me confident I'd be looked after and protected. Still, it hurt to leave my home and my last remaining family behind.

"What will happen to my father?" I asked.

Joe sighed. "Taylor, I'll always be honest with you, well, as much as I can. I think your father might find himself arrested. A deal has gone sour, he'll have to take the fall for that."

I turned in my seat to look at him.

"I don't know any of this," I said quietly.

Joe took hold of one of my hands. "I warned him this might happen. But you're not to worry, you'll be safe with us."

"I still don't understand why I had to leave."

"Because your father will need to save his own skin, as you Americans say. To do that, he might upset a few people. It's better this way."

"Where are you from?" I asked.

"Italy, although I've been here for many years now."

I gathered he was from Italy; I wanted to know *exactly* where. I also gathered he understood what I'd asked but had avoided answering.

I gently pulled my hand from his, using the excuse of wanting to get something from my purse so as not to offend him. It wasn't that I didn't want him to hold my hand, but I didn't know him.

"It was Mack's idea that you came with us," Joe said, surprising me. I noticed Mack glance in the rearview mirror at me.

"Well, I'm grateful to you both. I'll find somewhere to live and…Well, I guess I'll figure out what to do when I get there."

I had money in my own account; Momma had left me a sizeable amount in her will. I imagined it would be enough to buy an apartment and live on for a few years. I doubted I'd have to buy; perhaps I could lease and return home when everything was settled with Daddy.

I didn't appreciate the danger I was in, if I was in any at all, of course. I didn't doubt what Joe had said, but if Daddy was legitimate, surely he couldn't be sent to jail. I'd convinced myself that a month, tops, I'd be heading back to Texas.

Washington D.C. wasn't what I expected at all. At least where Joe lived. We were driven straight to his house and I wasn't sure I was happy about that. However, I had nowhere immediately to go. His daughter and son greeted us on the drive. In addition I counted five men, armed by the looks of it, either standing around the drive or by the door. All of them greeted Joe and Mack, one or two nodded at me. Evelyn introduced herself, and her warm smile and outstretched arms immediately put me at ease.

"Welcome, Taylor, we've been looking forward to meeting you. Now, you must be hungry," she said.

I was led to a vast kitchen and the smells of tomato sauce and herbs had my mouth watering immediately. I was shown to a chair and watched as Evelyn fussed around to dish up pasta. A loaf of bread was placed on a wooden board in the middle of the table and Joe took his seat at the head. Evelyn sat next to me. They asked me loads of questions about my life in Texas and had me chuckling at their insistence I tell them all about the many 'cowboys' I apparently met on a daily basis. Joey, Evelyn's brother, sat opposite, he didn't interact, and I put that down to shyness. He'd kept his head bowed, just occasionally answering if he was brought into the conversation.

It was clear that Joe had wealth but lived a humble life. Appliances were high-end but Evelyn was simply dressed.

Partway through the evening, I was startled to see a girl, about my age, join us. She didn't speak and her hands shook as she hesitated by the door. Evelyn introduced her sister, Maria, who gave me a very brief smile before silently leaving the kitchen without joining us.

"Maria has some *anxiety* issues," Evelyn told me.

"Is my being here going to make her worse?" I asked.

"No, it just takes her a little while to get to know people. She has the sweetest heart. After our mother died, she did too, inside," she answered.

I wasn't sure what to say to the news that her mother had died but I liked Evelyn, we had something in common that immediately bonded us. Although older than I was, and I wasn't sure by how much, she seemed very mature. I thought she might be a great friend.

After dinner, I was shown to a bedroom. It was basically furnished but very comfortable. I placed my case on the bed and sat for a while. I wasn't sure what the *plan* was and decided I'd speak with Evelyn in the morning. I couldn't stay with Joe and Evelyn forever and needed to decide what to do. I'd been away from home on my own before, well, with friends, but I'd never felt so alone as I did in that moment.

I wanted to be angry with my father; I wanted my momma. I changed into my sleep shorts and a tank before climbing between the sheets. I had a very restless night. It was warm and muggy, and many times I climbed from the bed and quietly paced the room, trying to settle my mind.

Chapter 5

It was two days later before I saw Mack again. He came to the house and invited me to join him for dinner. I was aware of the raised eyebrows and the smile from Evelyn. She clearly liked him, but I wasn't sure on the etiquette of spending an evening with him. Daddy would have freaked if I'd spent time with the *staff*, as he called them.

"I thought you might like to get out the house for a few hours," Mack said, as he opened the car door for me.

"Thank you. I feel quite disorientated. I just want to go home, but Joe and the family, have been amazing with me. I think I need to find somewhere to live, I can't stay in their house for too long."

I climbed into his car and he gently closed the door for me.

"Have you heard anything about my father?" I asked when he'd sat in the driver's seat.

He gently shook his head. "No, I'm sorry. I can ask Joe but, really, they're not *friends* as such, just business associates."

"Yet he has taken me into his home?"

"He has the kindest heart you'll ever find in a man of his caliber."

"What *caliber* is that?"

Mack just shrugged his shoulders before pulling into the traffic. We drove for a little while in silence, eventually ending up in Great Falls, as Mack informed me, and a small Italian bistro. It was the most authentic Italian restaurant I'd ever been to. We were immediately seated and the owner fussed around Mack as if he was someone important.

"So tell me more about you," I said, breaking a piece of bread and tentatively dipping it into a small bowl of oil and vinegar.

"Not much to tell really. I don't have family, I did, but…well, that's a long story. I work for Joe, which I guess you know."

"Doing security?" I asked, as the waiter placed some menus on the table.

Although we hadn't asked, he also placed a carafe of red wine and two glasses. I frowned. I wasn't old enough to drink alcohol, maybe, by being with Mack, the law didn't apply.

"That, and other things."

"Other things that you're not going to tell me about?" I asked, with a smirk.

I understood he wouldn't, or couldn't, tell me exactly what he did and, strangely, it didn't bother me. I think it would have, had I not already decided that I trusted Mack. In fact, I'd go as far as to say, I liked him, a lot. He was genuine, in that he didn't try to feed me any bullshit. He simply didn't answer when he couldn't, and I respected him for that.

"It's nice to get out," I said, once I'd ordered my meal.

"As much as I love Joe and the family, I'm sure you're going a little crazy right now."

"I need to plan what I'm going to do for the next month or so. I need somewhere to live, then sort out getting back home."

"Are you anxious to get back home?" Mack asked.

"I've never lived anywhere else. I was supposed to start college, but Daddy put a hold on that. I can't stay here, hiding out, or whatever the hell I'm doing."

"D.C. isn't so bad, you know. Maybe you can enroll in college here," he said, smiling at me.

"Maybe, but my friends are there, and my home."

A waiter placed some dishes of food on the table, and for a moment we sat and ate in silence. I was enjoying his company; I was also enjoying sneaking glances of him when he thought I wasn't. I remembered Carol's words about how handsome he was. A pang of homesickness washed over me. I wondered where she was, whether Monique was still at the house. I decided that when dinner was over, I was going to call and see who answered the telephone.

"You seem a million miles away, Taylor." Mack said, as he raised a forkful of veal to his mouth.

"I was thinking of Carol and Monique. I wonder if they're still at the house."

"If your dad is still there, then I'd imagine so."

"Why not me, then? If they're allowed to stay there, why couldn't I?"

"Like Joe said, if, and it's a big if, your dad gets arrested, who knows what he'll have to say to keep himself out of jail."

"Do you believe my momma was murdered because of my father?"

"It's possible. The driver, Rick wasn't it?"

I nodded my head.

"He's gone missing. Someone got him out of the hospital and has him well hidden because I know for fact your father has hunted the land for him. Only someone powerful could have taken him completely off-grid, without a trace."

"Powerful as in the government? They don't go around killing people...do they?"

He shrugged his shoulders as he continued to eat. I'd lost my appetite a little.

"Eat your dinner and let's try to put all that to the side for now. I want you to enjoy yourself for a little while," he said.

I sighed and picked up my fork. I'd ordered wild boar tagliatelle. I wasn't sure just how *wild* the wild boar was, but it tasted divine. I twirled the pasta around my fork before raising it to my mouth, at the same time I picked up my napkin. There was no way I wanted Mack to see me with sauce around my lips, or worse, on my cheeks.

I flitted between worry for my father, confusion, thanks to the lack of knowledge I had, and enjoyment at spending time with Mack. I wrestled internally with myself. I shouldn't be sitting in a bistro having a conversation with a man, while my father was in trouble. Then, there was a small part of me that appreciated that act of selflessness my father undertook. He sent me away for my protection, that couldn't, I hoped, have been easy.

Mack and I didn't stop talking, we laughed, and we told each other our fears and hopes. He was fiercely loyal to Joe and I admired that about him. By the time dessert was served, my jaw ached from talking more than I had in the past half a year.

"I don't want to head back just yet," I said, checking my watch to see it was only nine o'clock.

"What would you like to do?"

"Show me the sights for an hour?" I hadn't ventured out of the house in the few days I'd been in D.C.

He smiled and rose, I watched as he took his wallet from his pocket and laid some bills on the table. He then held out his hand. Without hesitation, I took it. He led me from the bistro to his car.

We drove for a little while, until he pulled into a small side road and then a parking lot. I had expected him to take me into the city; instead fields and trees surrounded us.

"Come on," he said, as he opened his door.

I stepped from the car and waited for him. He opened the trunk and then walked towards me with a jacket.

"Here, put this on, it's going to get a little chilly tonight."

I wasn't expecting to be out *all night* but I did appreciate the additional layer. I was fine in the car and the bistro, but out in the middle of nowhere, I felt the temperature drop.

Once again, he took hold of my hand and we walked a small path. Some parts weren't wide enough for the two of us and Mack would usher me in front by placing his hand on my lower back. My skin tingled at his touch.

We walked in silence and I thought. I'd had a couple of *boyfriends* as such, but no one captivated me the way Mack did. I wasn't sure what it was about him that drew me in so much. He was kind and considerate, for sure. He also had an aura of danger that didn't entice me, but certainly intrigued. He was a contradiction. All brawn but with a brain, a rare combination I believed.

"Why do you stick with security for Joe?" I asked.

We'd come to a clearing and any further conversation was momentarily halted. In front of me was a beautiful waterfall. Although not at full force, the sight took my breath away. The vibrant green grasses that grew between the rocks at the side of the fall, as if it cloaked it with a rich velvet fabric, took me aback.

"It's beautiful," I said.

Mack took my hand and pulled me to the ground. We sat side by side and I breathed in the clean, slightly damp air. Air so very different to the dryness of back home.

"In answer to your question. Joe took me in when I had no one. He told me I could do anything I wanted to. He was the only person that believed in, and supported, me. It was my choice to fight. I guess I had a lot of anger and it was a great way to channel that. I respect him, and he respects me. He's a great man, not necessarily always legal in what he does, but his heart beats for his family, extended as well as blood."

Mack spoke with such passion and devotion; I wanted to shed a tear.

"And yes, this is the most beautiful place I've ever been to," he added.

We fell silent again as I took in the view. On a summer's day, I'd love nothing better than to strip off and wade in the river, or to stand under the force of the waterfall and let it wash away my previous life. In that moment, I felt changed. I was sitting with a man that made my heart beat fast, his touch caused goosebumps to rise on my skin, and he was the only person that I wanted to spend time with since my momma.

I hadn't noticed the tear that gently rolled down my cheek until Mack swiped his thumb under my eye.

"Why the tears?" he asked.

I gently shook my head. "I was thinking of my momma, she would have loved it here," I said, giving him a half-truth.

He placed his arm around my shoulders and I gently fell into his side. It felt right; it felt comfortable.

"Absorb it all, she'll see it through you," he whispered.

Whether it was the waterfall, the humid evening, or being with Mack; I had a sense of belonging at that moment. Someone cared for me, I believed, I hoped. Did I still miss my home? Of course, but being with Mack had me forget about my loneliness and my father, and for that, I was thankful.

I wasn't sure how long we'd sat but I felt Mack stir.

"Did I fall asleep?" I asked, as I straightened up.

"I wouldn't say you were asleep, but you had your eyes closed and you snored a little."

I looked up at him. "I don't snore…do I?"

Mack laughed. "No, I was teasing. You closed your eyes though, and you sighed. I hope that was a sigh of happiness."

I smiled at him. "For a little while I didn't feel so alone."

He gave me just one nod before climbing to his feet and helping me to mine.

"I should get you home, Joe will be pacing the hallway, and then pretend he wasn't as soon as you walk through the front door. And I'll get an earful in the morning."

I laughed. "Joe doesn't even really know me, although I have to say, he and Evelyn are some of the nicest people I know."

I meant what I'd said, the family members were wonderful, and I loved spending time with Evelyn. I was always careful around Maria, though. She generally kept herself hidden away but if we met in the hallway, she'd give me a smile. She looked broken inside her mind. Her look was often haunting, as if her demons had taken over her body and thoughts. I felt terribly sad for her, and for the family, whose tormented eyes weren't as hidden as I think they would have liked them to be, whenever they looked at her.

We walked back to the car, and a sense of disappointment washed over me the closer to the house we got. Mack left the car and while I gathered my purse from the seat, he had opened the passenger door. He took my hand and walked me to the front door.

"Well, thank you for joining me for dinner," he said.

"I enjoyed myself. Maybe we can do it again sometime," I said. I wasn't one to wait around for a second invite.

Mack laughed. "Are you asking me on a date?"

"I am. Is that so wrong? I'm a modern woman, Mack. I've enjoyed myself; I think you have, too. So, let's do it again."

He nodded his head. "I have some things to do over the next day or so, but I'll give you a call."

Mack bade me a goodnight and he left to walk down the path toward his car. I smiled. It was refreshing not to have to fight him off for a goodnight kiss, or would I have fought him off? I wasn't sure.

Before I climbed into bed, I picked up the telephone on the night-stand. I opened my small address book and flicked through until I came to Daddy's office number. I dialed but stopped before I got to the last number. I wasn't sure of why I was so hesitant. I was still mad at him, at the way he'd sent me away, and I was upset that he hadn't made any attempt to contact me. I would have at least expected him to contact Joe to ask about me, but nothing. I placed the handset back in the cradle.

I flicked a little further until I came to a number for Carol. I decided to call her instead.

"Hello?" A voice I didn't recognize answered the phone.

"I'm sorry, I was trying to call Carol," I said.

"She's not here right now, can I give her a message?"

"Perhaps you could just let her know that Taylor called. If she has the time, could she call me back?"

"I'll be sure to let her know."

"Thank you."

I disconnected the call and could have kicked myself for not only asking who had answered the phone, but also for not leaving a number where she could call me back. I held the handset, just looking at the buttons for a little while, and wondering why I felt so unsettled. I flicked back to my father's name.

The phone rang, and continued to ring. Daddy always had voice-mail but after the sixth, or maybe it was the seventh, ring, an automated message informed me the call could not be connected.

Chapter 6

It was two days before I decided to try calling Carol again. That time there was no answer. Daddy hadn't called and I'd asked Joe if he'd heard any news.

"I haven't heard from him at all, Taylor. What I will do is contact someone I know and see if we can find any information for you, will that help?" he said.

I'd been sitting at the kitchen table with Joe and Evelyn.

"If you can, I'd appreciate that. As much as I'm thankful you've taken me in, I need to know what my future is. If I have to stay in D.C. any longer, I ought to look for my own apartment."

"You don't have to leave," Evelyn said.

"I know, but I don't want to be a burden. I was supposed to start college, Mack suggested I could look here, and if I can't find a course to suit me, I'll have to look further afield."

"Well, I do own some apartments if you really feel you want your own place. But let's wait and see what I can find out about your father," Joe said.

I smiled my thanks, still a little uncomfortable that I was in their house. They didn't know me, and as much as I appreciated their kindness, I felt displaced.

"Are you going out with Mack?" Evelyn asked, as I coated my lips with gloss.

"I am," I said, smiling at her reflection in the mirror.

"He's a good guy," she said, as she sat on the edge of my bed.

"I really like him. I'm not sure what would happen if I go home, though."

"I don't think Mack will leave here, if that's what you're hoping," she said.

"No, of course not. But I can't stay here, either…I don't think."

"Have you heard from your father?" she asked me.

"No, and I think that's strange. I tried Carol as well, she was our housekeeper, and a stranger answered the phone."

I put down my makeup and sat on the bed beside Evelyn.

"I'm scared, Evelyn. Momma was murdered, I've been sent

away, and I still don't really understand why. Joe and Mack said my father might have to take the fall for a deal that's gone wrong. But I don't get that. If he's done nothing wrong, then why?"

She sighed. "I don't know. Papa doesn't confide in me. You wouldn't be here if it wasn't for good reason, though. I know that much. Try not to think too much about it tonight. Go out and enjoy yourself," she said with a smile.

Evelyn was probably the kindest person I'd ever known. She was all the good people that had come and gone in my life, wrapped up in one Italian bundle. She was beautiful, yet she didn't realize it. I'd never heard her speak a bad word about anyone, she didn't complain, she just got on with life with a smile on her face. I would miss her terribly when I left.

We both smiled at each other when we heard the front door open and Joe greeted Mack. Evelyn raised her eyebrows slightly at me.

"Ready?" she asked.

I took a deep breath in and stood. "I sure am," I replied.

We walked down the stairs and his smile, as he saw me, had my heart fluttering.

"You look lovely, Taylor," Mack said, as I took the last step down.

"Thank you, although I'm sure you're just saying that."

I had hardly any decent clothes, but Evelyn had loaned me a white blouse to wear with dark jeans. It was a step up from t-shirts and hoodies. Perhaps I needed to visit a clothing store.

I noticed Joe stare at Mack, no words were spoken, but Mack slowly nodded his head as if he understood the silent communication.

"Shall we?" Mack said, opening the front door for me.

The evening was cool; a short rain shower had washed the humidity of the day away. I was thankful for that. I didn't want the blouse to be sticking to my sweaty body.

"So this is a date, yes?" Mack asked, as he opened the car door for me.

"Yep. Have you ever been asked on a date by a woman before?"

"Can't say that I have, now, buckle up. Don't want you messing with my windshield if I have to brake hard." He chuckled as he closed the door and crossed the front of the car to the driver's side.

We drove out of the city and I chuckled as he hummed along to a tune on the radio. Again the contradiction of him hit me. This hulk of a man was gently humming to a song that should be played at a wedding.

"Are you a bit of a romantic?" I asked.

He stopped his humming and looked briefly at me.

"I don't know, I'm just me. What is a *romantic* anyway?"

Not that I was experienced in all things 'men,' and I certainly didn't get my romance ideas from novels but I thought back to my parents.

"My daddy always complimented my mother, regardless of what she was wearing. He made a point to make her smile every day…" When my reality hit, it took me by surprise.

"But then he had affairs, lots of affairs. Why was my momma not enough for him?" I asked, completely changing the subject.

Mack sighed. "I can't answer that for you. I don't agree with affairs, if you're unhappy with someone, you should leave them, period. But he obviously loved your mom, so I don't understand why he'd seek out other women."

"I never asked him about it. I wanted to, I wanted to know just how much guilt he felt when she was gone. Did he have any remorse at all? I'm sure he knew that I was aware of what he did, Momma certainly was. I guess that begs the question, why did she put up with it?"

"I guess they didn't put as much importance on what your daddy did as you do. Plenty of people stay together through affairs, I couldn't. Betrayal is the worst thing anyone could do to me."

He seemed to bristle in his seat and I wondered if he'd already experienced that betrayal. I didn't believe it was my place to delve any further, though.

"So where are we heading to?" I asked.

"You mean you didn't plan anything? I thought you'd invited me on a date, shouldn't you have organized something?" he asked.

I stared at him. "Are we just driving aimlessly around, then?"

"Yeah, I'm waiting on you to tell me where to go."

His lips formed a smirk, the skin around his eyes crinkled into laugh lines. I punched his arm and he laughed.

"There's a restaurant I haven't eaten at, it looks good, though," he said.

We hadn't stopped talking for the whole journey. Eventually Mack pulled the car into a lot beside a small restaurant, another Italian restaurant I noticed.

"Do you only eat Italian?" I asked as I exited the car.

"Mostly, I guess Evelyn, and her mother before her, has spoiled me for choice," he said, taking my hand and leading me to the door.

The restaurant was modern in comparison to the bistro Mack had taken me to before. Small square wooden tables were spread out; most had two white, painted chairs around them. The walls were whitewashed, and the only things that saved the place from resembling the inside of a clinical looking operating room were the splashes of color. It looked as if someone had taken a paint-brush and flicked it against the wall. I stood and 'admired' the scene.

"I can't decide if it looks like art or a murder scene," Mack said, laughing beside me.

"I'm hoping you haven't seen that many murder scenes to know how they compare," I replied, raising my eyebrows at him.

He chuckled while we waited to be shown to our seats. I loved that he pulled the chair out for me to sit, not allowing the waiter to do so. I didn't love how his body had stiffened and his face hardened as he looked over my shoulder. I wanted to follow his gaze but he distracted me.

"How about a nice bottle of wine?" he said, thrusting the menu in front of me.

"Are you okay?"

"Sure. I'll let you choose the wine this time."

"I'm not old enough to order wine." He knew how old I was; perhaps he was more distracted than I thought.

He'd brought his attention back to me.

"Rules don't apply here," he said with a laugh. "Seriously, you look older and no one will want to see ID while you're with me."

I had no knowledge of wine. The list was full of Italian whites and reds. Mack seemed to know what he liked so I went along with his suggestions. I also asked for a jug of water. The waiter nodded his head, but I was more than aware that he kept looking at Mack rather than me.

"Sure is a lot of tension in this room," I said, sipping on the water that had been poured.

Mack cocked his head to one side, pretending to not know what I meant.

"If you'd rather leave and go elsewhere, I'm happy for that," I added.

"I'm sorry, it's fine. Someone I know, that's all. I want you to have a nice time. Shall I pour the wine?"

"Only if you're sure we're staying," I replied.

The waiter returned with menus, without speaking, he placed them on the table. I reached out and touched his arm.

"Before you rush off, are there any specials this evening?" I asked.

"Erm, yes, sorry."

He then proceeded to rattle off some dishes so fast, I had no chance of making a decision if I wanted one or not. I sighed and picked up the menu.

"I'll order from here, but thank you."

I studied the menu in silence for a few minutes, waiting for the tension to die down. I heard Mack clear his throat gently and I looked over the menu at him.

"Have you decided what you'd like?" he asked. I hadn't noticed him look at his menu.

I laid mine down. "Why don't you choose for me? I'm not really familiar with some of these dishes. The menu is mostly written in Italian, do you understand the language?"

"A little. When Joe is angry he shouts in Italian, I got to learn the cuss words quick enough."

He laughed, and I joined in. It was nice to be back on an even keel.

Mack waved for the waiter and placed our order, he poured me a glass of wine, and I raised it to him before I took a sip. A sip was all I managed.

I was jolted forward and my wine spilled down my blouse. Mack jumped up from his seat and before I had time to even mop the wine with my napkin, he held a guy, about the same size, by the throat beside me.

"Apologize," he said, his voice a little more than a growl.

I stood and as I did, I felt my legs tremble. I placed my hand on Mack's arm.

"It's okay, I'm sure it was an accident," I said.

The man being held laughed, although I wasn't sure that was in amusement. It sounded more as if it was a nervous laugh.

"It was no accident, Taylor. Now, apologize before I throw you through that fucking window," he said, turning his attention back to the man he was holding.

"Like your girl says, it was an accident. I'm sorry, Miss," the man said.

I wasn't sure of his level of sincerity and neither was Mack. He shoved him backward. I stood rooted to the spot as Mack walked over to a table; he laid both hands on the wooden top and leaned in close to an olive-skinned man.

"You have thirty seconds to vacate this place," he said, not as quietly as I think he had intended.

"Or?"

A challenge had been laid down. I heard the scrape of chairs as people left the restaurant. I wasn't sure what to do but gently backed away. I didn't hear Mack's reply, but I watched the man rise, throw his napkin on the table, and walk to the door. He looked over his shoulder directly at me; a shiver ran over my body at the smile he gave—a sickening smile.

"Miss?" I heard whispered in my ear.

I startled when a hand was placed on my arm. "Come this way, please," the waiter said in a gentle voice.

I hesitated at first, until I saw the guy that Mack had been holding begin to throw a punch. Mack deflected it easily enough and raised his fist. I didn't see if that fist connected with anything. The waiter pulled on my arm and I willingly jogged beside him into the kitchen.

"Miss, just wait here, yes?" he said in broken English. I nodded my head.

I heard a crash, as if a table had been upended, or maybe someone had fallen onto it. Glass smashed to the tiled floor. I covered my ears with the palms of my hands and closed my eyes. If I knew where I was, or could drive a car, I'd have left. As it was, I was stuck in the kitchen of a restaurant, while my date fought just a few feet away.

I wasn't sure how long it had been before I felt two hands around my wrists. They gently pulled my hands away.

"Taylor, are you okay?" Mack said.

I opened my eyes slowly. I was expecting to see bruises, or a cut, but there was nothing. I looking down to his hands, still holding my wrists. One hand had grazes across the knuckles.

"What was that all about?" I asked, finally looking back up at him.

"I'm so sorry. The guy is jerk and he was banned from here. He came to antagonize."

"But you said you hadn't been here before."

"Not to eat, I haven't. Joe owns this restaurant and that guy sitting at the table shouldn't have been here. He knew it, he sent his *boy* over deliberately to make a point. I showed him exactly the consequence of that."

I shook my head a little. "Couldn't you just have ignored him?"

"No, Taylor, this is my job."

"Your job is to *show people the consequences*?"

He placed his palms on my cheeks and lowered his head closer to mine. I could feel his breath on my skin and my heart started to race.

"Yes. But I didn't want to do that in front of you."

"But you did."

I so disliked that term: *I didn't want to do that in front of you*. People had choices; Mack chose to do what he did. He could have just walked away.

"I know, and I'm sorry, okay? Are you hungry? Let's get something to eat," he said.

I shook my head. "I think I'd like to go home…back to Joe's. I'd love to go home, but it's not possible, is it?"

He looked at me for a little while. He gave me a sad sort of smile; one where his lips didn't really move the muscles on his cheeks and the skin around his eyes didn't crinkle. I placed my hand in his and gave it a small squeeze. I hadn't enjoyed our date, but there was something about Mack that didn't have me run for the hills, either.

We walked to the car in silence and I smiled in thanks as he opened the door for me. I slid into my seat, hoping the grumbling in my stomach wasn't loud enough for him to hear.

Chapter 7

"Did you have a good evening?" I heard from the bedroom door. I turned to see Evelyn standing there.

"Not really. Come in, let me tell you all about it."

She walked into the room and settled at the bottom of the bed. I shuffled up and rested against the headboard, folding my legs underneath me. I enjoyed her company. She was like the older sister I never had, although I'd only known her for such a short time.

"What happened?" she asked.

"Mack got into a fight. I don't know why, or with whom, but it soured the evening, for sure. I didn't get to eat and I'm hungry," I said. As if on cue, my stomach grumbled.

"Well, let's get you something to eat. You know you can help yourself, don't you?" she said, standing from the bed. She held out her hand and I took it.

We walked to the kitchen and I was pleased to see it was empty. Joe often had a group of men lurking around at all times, one or two made me nervous. Evelyn indicated with her hand to sit.

"Let me help you," I said.

"No, sit, Taylor. I'm just going to heat up this sauce and put some pasta in a pan. I missed dinner so I'll eat with you."

"I want to help, though."

"Okay, you can get the bread, and there's some oil over there," she said.

I watched as she stirred the sauce and wondered when she'd bring up the subject of Mack. I decided to initiate the conversation.

"Evelyn, I might be talking out of turn here, but I'm just going to come out and say it. My father wasn't dealing with legal arms, I'm sure of that. And the fact your father had business dealings with mine suggests he isn't working legally either."

She stopped stirring the sauce but didn't turn to look at me. It took a few moments before she continued to check the pasta, when she was satisfied; she drained it and poured it into a bowl.

"Let's eat, Taylor. And we can talk."

She poured the sauce over the pasta and placed the bowl in the center of the table. She pulled a couple of small plates from a cupboard and grabbed some forks. Then she sat opposite me.

"What do you think Mack does?" she asked, spooning pasta on to the plates.

"Security, I know he also fights, I guess for money."

"You're correct, on both counts. Papa doesn't include me in his business, I've told you that before, but I know exactly what goes on. Mafia, Taylor, that's who my father is, that's who Mack works for. And, from what I understand, that's who your father is indebted to."

The forkful of pasta hadn't quite reached my mouth and I was glad, it had hung open at her bluntness. She chuckled.

"How was my father involved with the mafia? And is he indebted to your father?"

"He sold guns, as you know. And you were right, not always legally. He's not indebted to my father, but to another family. My father is the, how do you say…the negotiator for resolution."

I frowned at her, not understanding.

"There is a council, a collection of heads of families. My father sits at the top of that council. It seems your father didn't quite deliver on a deal, and my father is trying to resolve the issue before it gets out of hand."

"Mack told me your father was involved in property, my father wanted to buy some."

"What would you have said to him, had he told you the truth? You were supposed to be kidnapped, probably held to ransom, Taylor. Mack was trying to protect you from the truth."

My fork clattered to the table.

"I'm sorry for being so blunt, but I think you need to know the truth, as painful as is it. I was shielded for many years, my sister is sick because of our 'lifestyle,' I believe. I loved my parents; I especially love my papa. They are what they are, Taylor, but that comes with consequences."

"Rick was part of the mafia?" I asked.

"Not necessarily, he could have been paid, blackmailed, whatever. I doubt he's still alive, though. He would have been tasked to do something, then disposed of."

"How can you say that without emotion? I don't mean that to be rude, I just find…"

"Me lacking in compassion, maybe?" she finished my sentence for me.

"No. I don't know what I mean, to be honest. I'm sorry if I've offended you in any way."

She chuckled and gestured toward my fork. We ate in silence for a little while.

"So what do I do with Mack?" I asked.

"He likes you, a lot. How do you feel?"

"I like him, too. I'm only eighteen. I've had boyfriends, as such, but…"

"Mack will take good care of you, you have no worry there. He's a natural protector. And he was doing his job this evening. I don't know the circumstances, yet, but if Mack felt the need to fight, there would have been a very good reason. Trust him, always."

I dipped my bread in the remaining sauce; it was too delicious not to eat.

"Do you think I'll ever be able to go home? More importantly, am I safe here?"

"I don't know to the first question, but you are safe here. All the while you are under the protection of my father, no one will dare harm you."

"Yet the guy at the restaurant deliberately bumped into me."

"To rile Mack, I imagine. If there was an attempt to harm you, it wouldn't have been a bump in a restaurant."

I was finding it difficult to take in her words. I believed her, I trusted her, I just wasn't from the same world, and I had no idea how to deal with the knowledge she'd given me.

"I don't know what to do," I said.

"Do as Mack, and my father say, until this is all resolved. Promise me that, Taylor?"

"I promise, I will. I was there, remember, when he shot my momma. I don't think I'll ever get over that. I might seem as if I have, but inside, I'm in pieces most days. I close my eyes and I see her face. I want to cry but the tears won't come anymore, and I don't know why."

"Because you are a strong woman, Taylor. You'll never get over something like that, but you'll learn to live with it in your past."

I wasn't so sure about that but I smiled anyway. I helped Evelyn wash the dishes then headed back to the bedroom. I wanted some time alone to think about what she'd said. I hadn't been naïve enough to think my father was completely above board in everything he did, but to deal with the mafia was something else. The thought that I was in the same house as the mafia had me shiver. However, Joe, Evelyn, even Maria, were the nicest people I'd come across. Not so much young Joey who was always sullen but then, I rarely caught a glimpse of him. Maybe if I made myself believe they weren't the *mafia* mafia, not like the TV shows I'd watched, I'd be fine.

I didn't see Mack for a couple of days and I found myself missing him. I wasn't sure what the attraction was, he was older than me, of course, he was a good-looking man, but there was something that pulled me toward him. I had no idea how he felt, though. I would have hoped that, after our non-date, he would have been calling on me to check that I was okay, or to check that *we* were okay.

"Have you heard from Mack?" I asked Evelyn, as I helped her to hang some laundry on the line.

"I haven't but I know he's busy, he's not ignoring you. I think he's preparing for a fight, his last one, he tells Papa."

"Can he walk away from the fights?"

"Of course he can. It's his choice to fight, he isn't forced to," she replied, with a chuckle.

"I've been thinking, about this…mafia thing…"

Evelyn took the laundry basket from my hand and placed it on the floor. She led me to a small table and chairs, where we sat.

"I wondered when you'd want to talk a little more about it," she said.

"I just don't know what to feel. Should I be scared? Your family is so nice, I just can't get my head around it, to be honest."

She laughed. "It's not like the shows on the television. Well, I'm sure there are families that still behave that way, but Papa is different. He wants everyone who lives here to be safe, to have the best they can. Does he break the law? I'm sure he does, but I only know what I do from overhearing conversations, finding *things*, and being shunned by friends."

"Shunned by friends? I can't believe that."

"At school. People were wary of me and I wanted to know why. As you say, Papa is a good man, if they can't see that, it's not my problem."

"Where is Mack fighting?" I asked, changing the subject somewhat.

"You can't go, Taylor, Papa would forbid that. It's a group of horrible men, all betting on who is going to beat the other the best. It's not a nice environment."

"I don't think I'd want to go, but I'd like to see him. I miss him."

"Then there's nothing to say we can't go and watch him train, I'm sure he'd be pleased to see you."

My smile was broad at the thought of seeing him.

"Come on," Evelyn said. I hadn't thought she'd meant right then.

"I need to get ready…."

"You look beautiful. Now, while the house is empty we can sneak out," she said, giving me a wink at the same time.

"Will we get in trouble?" The thought of upsetting her father worried me.

"No, there's very little we'll ever get in trouble for."

Evelyn seemed to have a lot more freedom than I ever had, and I wondered if that was the power of her father.

I pulled on my sneakers and followed her from the house. She nodded at a guy that stood in the front yard, drawing hard on a cigar. He didn't speak but nodded back. As we walked, I noticed him a few paces behind us all the way, until we stopped by a door between two take-out stores. Evelyn tested the handle and smiled as the door opened. I wondered if she was expecting it to be locked. We climbed some stairs in a dark hallway. The smell of damp and sweat had my nose crinkle.

As we rounded the corner, I could hear grunts and curses, shouts and commands. I could hear the sound of boxing gloves hitting something and I hoped it wasn't a face.

Mack was in a ring that dominated the room. He hadn't noticed us and I watched as he trained with an older guy. Sweat ran down his body, every muscle was defined; his hair was stuck to his forehead. The old guy shouted instructions, holding pads in his hands, and the sound as Mack hit those pads with enough force to have the old guy stumble, resonated through my chest. My stomach clenched and it took a moment for me to understand it was with pleasure at the sight.

There was something primal about Mack at that moment. His total focus and concentration was on the man in front of him. It didn't seem he was aware of anything, or anyone, around him. As they moved around the ring, he could have easily seen me, but he didn't. He didn't take his gaze from his trainer at any point. I wondered; if I called out his name, would he even hear me?

I was transfixed. He moved so fluidly around the ring, everything was effortless. He bounced on his toes like a ballerina. He was a beautiful sight.

I fell in love that day.

Not with the boxer, not with the muscles, but with the man who could be so focused. Who could smile and growl at the same time; who could clearly knock the older guy over the ropes but held back a fraction just as his gloved fists connected with the leather pads. It shouldn't have excited me, but it did. It was the power of him; it was the force of nature that he was when in the ring and the gentleness he showed toward me.

I wanted to cry and I wasn't sure why.

When it looked as if Mack had finished his training, he allowed the older guy to pull off his gloves. His hands were taped and I noted one stained with red. I imagined his workout had opened up the grazes on his knuckles. Finally, he looked over to where we stood. His smile grew slowly. He ducked under a rope and jumped down from the ring. I stared at him as he walked toward us. It was only then that I noticed I was on my own. Evelyn had snuck off.

"Hey, what are you doing here?" he asked.

"I…Sorry, I'm not sure I should be. I just wanted to see you," I said, stammering through my sentence.

"You can be here if you want to, although I'm not sure I like the way some of the guys are staring at you right now," he said, looking around to a group of men standing to one side.

"If I'm causing a problem, I can leave," I said.

"No, I'm teasing. They know not to make a move on you," he replied a little louder than necessary. "Let me take a shower and then we can do something if you like, maybe take a ride somewhere?"

"I'd like that."

"Come on."

He took my hand and led me to a locker room. I hesitated at the door, not sure I should be in there. Mack laughed and pulled me forward. He indicated to a bench and I sat. I watched as he grabbed a towel, nothing else, and walked around a tiled wall. I closed my eyes to the sound of a shower running in the hopes my imagination wouldn't run wild. It didn't work.

I inhaled deeply to quell my racing heart. I held my breath as he walked back into the room with just a towel around his waist.

"You might want to close your eyes," he said, as he opened a locker.

I placed my palms over my face, but no matter how hard I tried, I couldn't stop my fingers parting ever so slightly. I wanted to giggle. He had the tightest, nicest ass, I'd ever seen.

I watched as he pulled on some jeans, and then a t-shirt. He rubbed the towel over his hair, leaving it standing on end in places. Then he walked toward me and pulled my hands from my face.

"It's really good to see you," he said, sitting astride the bench and facing me.

I looked at his hand. Then I did something I hadn't planned. I raised his hand to my lips and gently kissed the broken skin on his knuckles. I heard his breath catch and I was too scared to look at his face. Mack pulled his hand away and placed it on my cheek, he slid it into the hair at the side of my head. At that point, I looked up at him.

His eyes had darkened and his lips were parted. He shuffled closer and yet again, I held my breath.

Our knees touched and I felt him use his free hand to lift my leg and place it over his, I voluntarily did the same with my other leg. He wrapped his arm around my waist and pulled me closer still. He lowered his head to mine, pausing just close enough for me to feel his breath on my lips. I closed my eyes and waited.

"Give me permission, Taylor," I heard him whisper.

I didn't speak but placed my hand on the back of his head and pushed it closer, it was all the *permission* he needed. I parted my lips as his tongue swiped over them. His kiss was gentle, tender, until I curled my fingers slightly, digging my nails into the back of his head. He gripped my hair as he devoured my mouth. He took the air from my lungs, my stomach clenched with desire, and my heart beat a rapid rhythm.

I'd been kissed before, but never like that. There was no

awkwardness, no clashing of teeth. It was all passion and lust yet the fact he'd asked my permission, it was full of respect as well.

I could feel his hand tighten further in my hair, painfully so. His other gripped my thigh. When he moaned, I lost it. I curled my legs around his waist and pushed myself into his groin. The pulsing between my legs matched the beating of my heart. I kissed him back hard, struggling to drag enough oxygen into my lungs as I did.

It was the opening of the locker room door that had us, reluctantly, pull apart. Embarrassment flowed over me and I pulled my legs from around his waist. Mack had other ideas, without looking to see who had stepped into the room, he simply told them to, *'fuck off.'* I heard a chuckle and the door softly close again.

"Come home with me, Taylor," Mack said, his voice low and gravelly.

"I..."

"What?" His eyes searched my face for an answer.

"I haven't done this before," I whispered.

He gently nodded his head. "Then come back and let me kiss you properly."

If I had the strength, I would have widened my eyes. Unfortunately, he'd kissed all reason and ability to from me; I nodded my head.

Mack slid my legs gently from around his waist and then stood. He smiled down at me while he slipped his feet into sneakers. Without a word, I followed him to his car.

All the while he drove, he held onto my hand. Every now and again, he would glance my way and give me a smile. I had no idea where he lived but as the minutes ticked on, my nerves kicked in. I wanted to remove my hand from his and wipe my sweaty palm on my jeans. Or perhaps it was to hold my leg down and stop the shaking.

We pulled onto the drive of a large house. I stared up at the building.

"Do you live here?" I asked.

"No, thought I'd just turn up at some random house," he said with a laugh. "I have the top floor, it's apartments now. I bet it was a magnificent house in its day, though."

I let out a nervous laugh and waited until he opened the passenger door for me. He took my hand and led me up the four steps to a large, black painted front door. Once through, we took the stairs to his apartment.

He opened the apartment door and pushed it to one side, letting me walk in first. I was surprised by the size and décor. I wasn't sure what to expect, I guess, but the neatness, the modern interior, wasn't it.

"It's a lovely apartment," I said, unsure what to say to cover my nervousness.

"Thank you, I lease it from Joe. He owns a lot of property. I like it here, it's quiet and the neighbors are friendly."

He walked past me and I followed into a neat kitchen. He set the coffee machine on and then leaned against the counter.

"Come here," he said.

I stepped closer. "Nothing will happen that you don't want to happen, okay?" he said.

I wanted to speak but it seemed words had left me. I nodded instead. I looked up at him and knew he'd take care of me. His features were soft, the opposite of the man I'd watched in the boxing ring. His posture was unthreatening, his shoulders relaxed, but the obvious bulge in the front of his jeans caused those nerves to rack up a level.

"Are you nervous?" he asked quietly.

"Yes."

"Good. Do you want a coffee?" His question took me by surprise.

"No, I want you to kiss me."

He reached forward and pulled me toward him. As he wrapped his arms around me, a sense of comfort washed over me. He turned so I had my back to the counter, and then I squealed as he lifted me so I was sitting on it.

"Same height, a bit easier," he said.

He kept his hands on my hips and stared at me.

"Can I touch you?" I asked. I struggled to hold his gaze.

"Where do you want to touch me?" he asked, I noticed that gravel back in his voice.

I slid my hands under his t-shirt and up his stomach. I felt his muscles tense as I did. Yet I didn't think that was from vanity, his body was reacting to my touch. My hands ran over his chest and I felt him take in a sharp breath. Before I could do anything else, he whipped off his t-shirt. I'd seen him in the gym but close up, he was stunning. The desire to kiss his skin overwhelmed me. I leaned forward and let my lips trail over his chest and up to the base of his neck. He raised his head as I brushed over the day old stubble under his chin.

Eventually I found what I was looking for, his lips. I ran my tongue over the lower one, tasting him. He parted his lips gently and I covered his mouth with mine. I wanted him. I wanted to feel his skin against mine. I pulled my head back and my t-shirt over my head. I unclipped my bra and watched as his gaze slowly lowered from my face to my breasts. I took his hands from my hips and placed them on my chest. I knew Mack would want me to lead, he'd want that permission, and I was giving it.

His hands slid over my breasts and his palms grazed my nipples. He rotated his hands gently, adding more and more pressure. I placed my hands on the countertop behind me and leaned slightly back. He stepped closer; close enough for me to feel his erection through his jeans. I wanted to grind myself against him, to ease the ache that had settled between my thighs.

Mack slid his hands around my back and pulled me straight.

"I told you I wanted to kiss you properly," he whispered, as he nuzzled my neck.

"I want you to," I replied, aware of how 'breathy' I sounded.

Mack lifted me from the counter; I wrapped my legs around his waist and my arms around his neck. He carried me into his bedroom and gently laid me down on his bed. He reached down and undid the button to my jeans, and then he paused and looked at me. I nodded. He lowered the zipper and hooked his fingers in the loops, slowly pulling my jeans to my ankles. I kicked off my sneakers, and then the jeans.

Mack climbed on the bed and straddled me. He held both my hands and raised them to the side of my head. He kissed the side of my neck, from my ear to the dip in my throat. He ran his tongue down my throat and chest, across until he circled one nipple.

I'd made out with guys before, but I'd never had the feelings coursing through my body that Mack seemed to produce. I wanted to arc my body and force my nipple into his mouth. I needed more from him.

Before I could do anything, Mack sat back up, his knees astride mine. He shuffled back, lowering his head to kiss my stomach. At the same time, he hooked his fingers at either side of my panties and lowered them. I wanted to cover myself; I didn't get the chance. Mack ran his tongue through my pubic hair and when he circled my clitoris, I squealed, again.

I lowered my hands to my sides and gripped the bedding. I dug my heels into the bed and raised my hips slightly.

"Oh, God, fuck," I whispered, as his lips closed around my clitoris and he gently sucked.

The vibrations as he laughed clashed with the static coursing over my body. When he swiped his tongue over my opening, I cried out. There was a part of me so very embarrassed that his mouth was over my most intimate area. There was another part that had me forcing my legs as far apart as I could, bearing in mind he was straddling me. The wetness I could feel between my thighs was as arousing as the tongue licking at it.

It was disappointment that flowed over me when Mack raised his head. I could see my wetness glistening on his chin. He crawled up my body and kissed me hard. I could taste and smell myself on him. He lowered until he was lying on top of me; I hooked my heels over his legs, wishing he wasn't wearing his jeans.

I pulled his head back, releasing my mouth so I could speak.

"Mack, I want you to…" I struggled with the words.

"Only when you're ready, Taylor," he replied.

"I'm ready, I've been ready for the past half hour or so," I said forcefully.

He propped himself up on his elbows and looked at me. "Emotionally, Taylor. When you're ready, emotionally. I'll make you come, I won't be that fucking mean, but nothing more."

He rolled to one side and slid his hand over my stomach and between my thighs. I wanted to cuss him out, or punch his chest even, but all thought of violence left me when he inserted one, then two, fingers inside me.

Mack did as he promised, he made me come so hard tears left my eyes and rolled down my cheeks. He kissed each eye as I came down and tiredness swept over me.

Chapter 8

I woke naked, but with a sheet over me, and disorientated. For a moment, I just looked around the room, gathering my thoughts. I was alone but I could hear Mack in another room. I rose and wrapped the sheet around my body. I had a plan. Mack had thought I wasn't emotionally ready to lose my virginity, but I was. Although I hadn't known Mack that long, I'd never been as sure about a decision as I was then.

I walked into the living and saw him look up at me. He was sitting on the sofa in just his jeans, and he held a telephone to his ear. He smiled as he watched me slowly let go of the sheet and it pooled around my feet. I took a few steps closer to him but not close enough so he could reach out and touch me.

I feigned confidence as I ran my hand over my stomach and let my fingers trail close to my opening. His smile grew wide while he continued with his conversation. I slowly lowered to my knees, parting my legs so he could watch. I ran my fingers over myself and coated them with my juices. I got his full attention when I inserted one inside me.

"I need to call you back," he said, replacing the handset on the telephone without waiting for an answer.

"What are you doing?" he asked, as he shuffled so he sat on the edge of the sofa.

"Showing you that I am emotionally ready. I want you to take my virginity, Mack. I've never asked that of anyone before, but it's you I want." My voice hitched with desire.

He rested his forearms on his knees and leaned forward. He studied me intently, watching every movement my fingers made.

"Make yourself come for me," he whispered.

I could do that just on his command alone. His tone of voice cut through me, it was low and demanding, gruff, and had my stomach clench. I closed my eyes and just allowed the feelings I was producing to wash over me. I thought of him, I inhaled my scent; I listened as his breathing became more rapid and the crackle as he moved on the leather sofa. It was when I heard the sound of a zipper being lowered that I opened my eyes.

Mack had his hand down the front of his jeans; he was massaging himself.

"I want to watch you as well," I said.

He stood and let his jeans fall to his ankles. He was naked underneath, and I had to catch the gasp from leaving my lips at the sight of him. Mack was very much all *man*. He sat again and his hand clasped around his cock. Very slowly he ran that hand up and down his length. I found myself mirroring his pace. My mouth watered at the thought of tasting him. I imagined the skin on his cock to be silky smooth; the saltiness of his pre-cum would dissolve on my tongue. The more I thought of him, the more I ached for him to be inside me.

As his hand moved faster, so did my fingers. I could feel the heat travel through my body and my cheeks reddened. My mouth was dry, my heart beat rapidly, and I bit down on my lower lip to stop the moan that built in my chest.

"Let go, Taylor," he said quietly.

I watched as he fisted his cock faster. "Fuck me now, Mack," I said, trying to speak evenly through the panting.

Mack leapt from the sofa, at the same time I lowered myself to the floor. He knelt between my legs and inserted his finger alongside mine, stretching me.

"Are you ready for me?" he asked. I nodded my head and pulled my hand away.

Mack guided himself inside me, very slowly and gently. I expected to feel pain; that was something my girlfriends had told me. It would hurt, I'd bleed, they said. I felt none of that. The only word I could think of for what I felt was contentment. As Mack lowered his body to cover mine, I smiled up at him. He rocked his hips against mine, I could feel every inch of him inside me; it wasn't enough, though.

I wrapped my legs around his, opening myself further to him. As he pushed deeper inside me, I did wince then. I took a deep breath in and willed my muscles to relax. Mack slowed. I placed my hands either side of his head.

"Don't stop," I whispered before I kissed him.

I cried out his name, I clawed at his back. I tightened my legs around his and raised my hips from the floor. I could hear the blood rush past my ears and I could feel the thudding of his heart against my chest. Sweat formed on my brow and my cheeks were so heated the sweat that dripped from him should have been sizzling.

He whispered my name over and over, and each time my stomach clenched further and my pussy pulsed more. I lost track of time, but eventually I couldn't contain the ache, dampen the heat, or settle the butterflies in my stomach. My orgasm hit me like a freight train; way more powerful than anything I'd been able to produce myself.

Mack fucked me faster through it. Our bodies slid against each other's, and when his mouth crashed down on mine, and I absorbed the growl that emitted from the depths of his chest, I knew he was about to come. He breathed hard through his nose; his body shuddered and tensed. Eventually his kiss became gentler; his body lowered to mine and he wrapped an arm around my neck. He pulled his lips from mine and rested his head in the crook of my neck. We stayed that way, in silence, for what seemed like the longest time.

"Are you okay?" I heard.

"I'm more than okay, although you're going to have to move soon, I have a cramp in my leg."

Mack laughed and rolled to the side. He dragged the sheet from his side and placed it over us. He pulled me close, wrapping his arms around me and kissing me on the forehead.

"Seriously, how do you feel?" he asked.

"Wonderful, sore, like I've been ten rounds with you in that boxing ring, but...I don't know the words, really. I feel good, very good."

"We've been a little irresponsible though, we didn't use any protection."

"If I get pregnant, you're just gonna have to marry me then. I'm a good Texas girl, my daddy will shoot you, if you don't," I teased.

Mack laughed out loud. "I'd marry you even if you weren't pregnant," he whispered.

I stilled in his arms. He was joking, I was sure.

"We need to get cleaned up," he said and I sighed.

"Do we? Why can't we stay like this for the whole day?"

"Mmm, that doesn't sound like a bad idea. But you might need to let Evelyn know where you are, so she can cover for you."

"Can you call her?"

"I can dial the number, then you can lie to her," he said, giving me a wink. He pushed himself up from the floor. I rested on one elbow and cocked my head to one side.

"I don't tell lies, pass me the telephone."

Mack dialed the number and handed me the handset. I prayed that it would be Evelyn who answered the phone and not Joe.

"Hello?" I breathed a sigh of relief at the sound of Evelyn's voice.

"Hi, I'm at Mack's. He suggested that I call you, lie, so you could cover for me. But, here's the thing. We just had sex and I'd like to stay here for a little while longer, can you cover for me?"

I wasn't sure who laughed the loudest, Mack or Evelyn.

"I won't lie for you, but I'm sure you just told me that you're at the college looking at design courses, then you're off to the library to do some research on what you need to do to get into the college, okay?"

"Sounds good to me. Thank you, Evelyn, I really do appreciate your support."

"Anytime. Give my love to Mack, won't you? Let him know if he hurts you, that will get repaid tenfold."

I laughed as I replaced the handset. Mack shuffled to sit behind me. He wrapped his arms around my chest and I rested back into him.

"You are one sassy woman, I think I just fell in love," he said. I hoped he wasn't teasing that time.

"She said, if you hurt me, you'll get paid back tenfold. I assume she meant she'll do the hurting," I said.

"I'm sure she would. She a tough woman, that one."

"Does she have a boyfriend?"

"That is a long and tragic story. A story only she should tell. Now, I'm hungry, for food."

"I'm hungry, not for food. Flip a coin?"

Despite my soreness, we had sex again. Mack lay on his back and I straddled him. I enjoyed it more because I got to control the speed, the depth. I got to tease him, play with his balls as I rode him. As I watched the expression on his face as he came, I got to fall harder in love.

———————————

I had showered and dressed, albeit reluctantly, and was sitting in the kitchen watching Mack cook. Like Evelyn, it was a pasta dish that he'd put together. I guessed the sauce that he took from the fridge, stored in a plastic container, came from Evelyn, and it smelled delicious. Mack dished up two bowls and we sat at the breakfast bar and ate. We chatted about our lives, mine back in Texas and prior to losing my mother, and his in D.C. He avoided talk of family and I didn't push him. To him, his family was Joe and I guessed whatever had come before that had been too painful for him to want to recall. He told me of his plans for his last fight and when I asked if I could attend, he absolutely forbade me to.

"I like forceful Mack," I said, finishing my meal.

"Good. Taylor, one thing you need to know about me. I'm not a chauvinistic pig but I live in a world where protecting you will be in the forefront of my mind…"

He held up his hand as I opened my mouth to speak.

"You're not in any danger, okay? But my world is different to yours. Not so different to your father's, but you weren't aware of that. I need to know I have your complete trust in any decision I make, even ones you don't agree with."

"Can I get an example of a decision I might not agree with?" The sassiness was bubbling away inside me.

He fought hard to contain the smirk. "If I say you can't come to a fight, you can't, no argument. If I say you need a driver, or you need someone with you if I'm not, there's no question on that. I won't suffocate you, Taylor, I won't contain you, but I will protect you and you might not appreciate that all the time."

"Mmm, I think I can live with that."

I wanted to take back my words. Did he think I wanted to live with him? Well, when I thought about it…

"Good. Now we need to tell Joe."

"Tell him what, Mack?"

We'd had sex, twice, I was hoping for more before the day was out, but what exactly did I mean to Mack?

"That you'll move in with me, and we'll get married at some point."

"Is that a proposal? Because if it is, that was shit."

Mack laughed. "No, just a promise for something in the future, if you want it, of course."

"I'll have to think about that. Now, do you want me to help clear these dishes?"

"No, I want you to get naked in my bed." Mack raised his eyebrows at me.

"Are you trying to coerce me? Do you think all this sex might have my brain scrambled enough to give in to your shit proposal?"

"Absolutely. I could fuck you into submission anytime, Taylor, but I like your smart mouth," he said with a wink.

I was pretty sure he could, smart mouth or not. I pursed my lips and frowned, as if deliberating his request. I took a deep breath and let it out slowly.

"Okay, on this occasion I concede. You may have me naked in your bed, but don't think for one minute you'll get your own way all the time," I said.

"I've no doubt you will fucking challenge me, baby."

He slid from his stool and picked me up. I laughed as he carried me to his bedroom and after he'd placed me back on my feet, he undressed me.

He didn't fuck me; he made love to me. He was gentle and considerate. He whispered that he loved me. I hadn't been a believer of 'insta-love.' I'd known Mack for just a couple of months in total, but there was no doubt what I felt about him. I told him that I loved him back.

We were sitting in his car outside Joe's house. The sun had set a while ago and Mack had already taken a call inquiring on where I was. I wasn't sure Joe had been convinced by Evelyn's story and my nerves kicked in.

"Do I smell of you?" I asked.

"I'd fucking love that, but no," Mack replied, laughing.

"What if Joe knows?"

"So what? You're allowed a boyfriend, Taylor. He'll get pissed at me, but not you."

"Why would he get pissed at you?"

"Because he'll say we don't know each other well enough. He'll say I've got to concentrate on this fight, he'll know, though, that I don't introduce anyone to him unless I'm deadly serious about them."

I frowned at his choice of words as he got out of the car and opened my door. He took my hand and walked me toward the front door. He knocked, despite the fact both he and I had a key. And of course, the miserable guy was stationed at the front door.

When Joe opened the door, we watched as he folded his arms over his chest, his face was stern.

"Yes?" he said, looking directly at Mack.

"Joe, I want to introduce my girlfriend. Well, she's a little more than a girlfriend. When she's ready, she's going to move in with me, and we'll get married."

I saw Joe raise his eyebrows. Evelyn stepped up behind him; Maria was wringing a dishtowel in her hand.

"You'll do no such thing. Both of you, in my office, now."

I wanted to cry. I wanted to crumple to the floor, and I wanted to shout that I was my own person, able to make my own decisions. I opened my mouth until I saw Evelyn gently shake her head. I followed Joe into his office.

"You will not move in with him, and then marry him, Taylor,"

Joe said. He held up his hand to stop the words about to leave my mouth.

"You will marry him before you move in with him," he said.

I blinked a few times, not entirely sure that I'd understood what he said.

"As for you? What the fuck do you think this is, huh? She's a woman with class, and you want to treat her like a… like a…. what's the fucking word?"

"Cheap date?" I heard behind me. Evelyn covered her mouth to quell the laughter.

Joe waved his hand to usher his daughter away.

"Whatever, you will not disrespect her all the time she is under my care. You have my permission to marry her, of course, but you will treat her the way I expect any member of my family to be treated."

Joe turned his attention to me. "Do you want to marry him? Live with him?"

"Erm, yes. I know it's kind of fast and he hasn't proposed in a way I'd accept, yet."

"Then it is done. He will propose properly to you and you have my blessing."

Joe's smile was infectious. I beamed, Mack laughed, and Evelyn hugged me. However, it was all tinged with sadness.

"What about my father?" I asked Joe.

"Tomorrow, Taylor, we talk about that. Tonight we drink wine and celebrate."

From watching Mack in a gym to sipping wine with my 'adoptive' family, it felt like months in between. I was caught up in the celebration to the point that I started to believe I was getting married and this was an engagement party. I accepted congratulations; all that was missing was a ring on my finger. It was later that night that reality hit.

The 'marriage' conversation had started as a joke. It wasn't meant to be serious. Not that I wouldn't have accepted Mack's proposal at some point in the future, should we still be together, but I felt we had been blindsided by Joe. Maybe it was an Italian thing, or maybe it was something else. Perhaps it was convenient that I marry Mack, or at least was seen as his partner. Was this part of their protection of me? Sadness washed over me, or maybe I'd drunk too much wine and was overthinking the whole thing.

What I would do, though, was have a proper conversation with Mack as soon as I could.

I slept fitfully that night and as soon as the sun was up, I rose, showered, and dressed. I crept downstairs knowing that at least Evelyn would be up.

"Good morning, did you sleep?" she asked, as I walked into the kitchen.

"Not really. I need to speak to Mack, I think everyone got a little carried away last night. We're not engaged, or anything. This marriage thing, it was a throwaway comment and I'm not sure where I stand."

"Sit, have a coffee and talk me through it all," she said. She placed a cup on the table and poured from the coffee pot.

"Do you love him?" she asked.

"I've only known him for a short time…"

"I didn't ask that. Do you love him?" she smiled as she spoke.

"Yes, but should I?"

"Why do you question it?"

"Because I've only…"

"Taylor, what does time have to do with anything? Do you think you meet someone and grow to love them?"

"I…I don't know."

"Mamma met my papa when she was a very young girl and knew she would marry him one day. Time is meaningless when the heart wants something, Taylor."

"What if he doesn't love me?"

"Then he would not have presented you to us in the way he did. It's our custom, a custom he has adopted."

"I don't really know anything about him. He doesn't know

anything about me, in fact, I don't know anything about me anymore."

I could hear my voice begin to hitch.

"What do you need to know to confirm how you feel? His parents abandoned him as a child. Why? Neither he, nor us, know. He has no desire to know, so he can't give you any information on his parents. He has no siblings he's aware of. I can tell you of the man I know, he's kind, considerate, caring, fiercely loyal, and when he loves, Taylor, he loves with his whole being, not just his heart."

"What do I do?"

"What you already planned to do. You court, you spend time together, and then you plan your future if there is to be one."

"I need to talk to my father. Can I do that?"

"I'm sure you can. Why don't you go and have your chat with Mack, he'll be at the gym already, then we'll speak with Papa about your father."

I thanked her for the chat, wondering how I was so lucky to be taken care of by such a wonderful woman. Then I left and headed for the gym, trying to remember the exact route. Miserable Man, as I'd nicknamed him, followed a few paces behind, so I was thankful I wasn't at least going to get lost.

The gym was empty except for Mack. He was sitting on a bench in the middle of the room facing the door. He wore a tank top and shorts, and I wondered if he was about to start his training or had long since finished. He smiled when he saw me but didn't speak. I walked across the room and straddled the bench, facing him.

"We need to talk," I said.

"That we do," he replied, and my heart sank a little.

"I want you to know that I think Joe might have gotten a little carried away and if you want for us just to be friends, date, or whatever, for a while, that's fine…."

I didn't get to finish my story before his lips closed on mine, cutting off my words. When he'd finished kissing me, he sat back.

"I'm going to marry you, Taylor, if you'll have me. I made that decision some time ago. Now, you need to decide if you feel the same, and no matter what, everything will always be according to you. You decide when you're ready for me."

I placed my palm on his cheek and smiled at him.

"I'm ready for you, Mack. I was born ready. I just wanted to be sure you didn't feel this whole thing has exploded out of control. I need to speak to my father, Joe is going to see if that's possible."

His smile was wide. I climbed from the bench, not wanting to disturb his training any longer.

"Oh, you need to take me on a proper date, the last one was shit. I'd appreciate if you didn't beat anyone up this time."

He laughed as I made my way back to the door. The old guy I'd seen the previous time I'd visited, met me. He had a cigarette in his mouth and he cocked his head at me.

"I'm going, I'm not going to distract him from his training," I said, ducking under his arm. I heard the cackle of laughter follow me down the stairs.

That day I made an appointment with Evelyn's doctor and put myself on the pill. No matter what our future was, a child wasn't something I wanted at that early stage.

***

It was another two days later that I saw Mack again. I'd pestered Joe as to why the silence and was given various reasons, none of which made sense. I wanted to walk to his apartment but knew I'd never remember the way and Miserable Man, who stood guard at the front door, wouldn't help me, even after I tried to bribe him with cigarettes that I'd bought from the local store.

I was asleep when I felt the bed dip. It startled me awake. The moon was still high in the sky; it wasn't morning. I fumbled around to turn on the bedside lamp and then covered my mouth with my hand to stop the gasp from leaving.

Mack sat on my bed with a graze across his cheek and cut on his upper lip.

"What happened?"

"I won my last ever fight, Taylor."

"You're gonna tell me that if I think you look bad, I should see the other guy, aren't you?"

He chuckled. "Nah, you don't want to see the other guy, he's a mess."

"Is that why you've been missing?"

"I haven't been missing, but I've been training and you are way too much of a distraction."

"So you won?"

"I did, I always win. Which is why I am bowing out now."

I shuffled closer to him. "I missed you."

"I missed you, too. But I have some news that I think you might not like. Your father is missing. We don't know where he is. He's alive, but…"

"Wait, hold up. He's missing but you know he's alive?" I was more alert at that point than I had been.

"He checked in, he ran. Joe told him not to. We can't help him now that he's decided to take his chances on his own."

"Mack, you have to tell me what you know."

"Your dad made a deal with a family. He took their money but then couldn't deliver on the goods. He didn't have the money to pay back, and they want it. The feds offered him a deal, if he gave evidence on the illegal purchase of guns, they'd go easy on him. Joe offered to help him solve his problem directly with the family. He has decided to turn both offers down."

I slumped back against the headboard, his words swimming around my head.

"I don't understand. Why didn't he just pay the money back?"

"Because he didn't have it. Your momma was the wealthy one, she didn't want to continue to support his activities, I guess. You own the house, your father tried to sell it but he couldn't."

"Why don't I know this?"

"I can't answer that. All I can do is tell you what I know so far."

"Can you find him?"

"Not if he doesn't want to be found, baby. I'm sorry."

I wanted to cry but I guessed the news was just too much to take in.

"His dealing with the 'family' is what killed my mother, wasn't it?"

Mack nodded his head.

"I don't know how to deal with all this. I mean, you're part of that world. I just…"

"Taylor, I'm not part of *that* world. What we do here is something else…"

"I understand that, I do, but…"

"But, what?"

"How do I know you're safe? How do I know I won't end up with a bullet in my head, just like my momma did?"

"I'd die protecting you, Taylor."

"You see, that's what I can't have. Can you understand that?"

"No, I don't. I won't let you get hurt. I asked you to trust me, I need you to do that."

"If I can't?"

"Then we won't make it."

His statement hung in the air like a time bomb waiting to explode.

"I love you," I said quietly.

"Then trust me, Taylor. Believe in me, and *this* family. I'm begging you to."

He reached forward and pulled me into his arms. I wanted to, so badly, I needed to because the thought of not being with him hurt more than the risk I knew I was taking. I nodded into his chest and heard his sigh.

"I meant what I said, I'd die protecting you, and I'm sure not planning on dying any time soon."

Chapter 9

A week passed and Mack and I saw each other every day. I sat with Joe and discussed my father, he pretty much confirmed everything that Mack had told me. He promised that he'd look after me and that I was part of his family. I voiced every concern I had and I asked him for one favor. I asked him to find Rick and to kill him. Joe didn't answer verbally, but he nodded his head.

"Revenge, Taylor, isn't always as tasteful on the tongue as you might think. But I will do this one thing for you. If you will do one thing for me."

"What?" I asked.

"You trust in us, especially Mack."

I didn't have to think, I nodded, and our meeting was concluded.

It was a month later that I was given an envelope. I was sitting in Joe's home office when he presented it to me. I slowly opened it.

It contained a photograph. I stared at that photograph for what seemed an age. A lone tear dripped on to the image, not in sadness at what I was looking at, but at the thought of why Rick was lying on the ground with a bullet hole in the center of his forehead.

"Mack did that for you," Joe said. "Mack killed that man because it was what you wanted of us."

I closed my eyes at the thought, but I was in too deep to ever think of letting that knowledge affect me.

"You were wrong, Joe. Revenge does taste so sweet, like the honey my momma always bought from the nearby farm. Thank you."

I stood and left the photograph on the table, I had no need for it. That day, Miserable Man drove me to Mack's apartment.

"What is your name?" I asked him before I left the car.

"Paulo, everyone calls me Paul."

"Well, thank you for the ride. Now, you're sure Mack is home?"

"Yes, I called him myself."

I nodded and climbed from the car. I rang the doorbell to Mack's apartment and waited until I heard the click of the lock as it was disengaged. Mack opened the door and his surprised look soon faded into a smile.

"Hey, what are you doing here? I was going to pick you up you later," he said, opening the door wider.

I watched him glance at the car, and then nod. The vehicle left.

"I wanted to surprise you," I said. "And since I'm going to be living here at some point, I thought I might take some measurements. We're going to need some new furniture."

I walked up the stairs and he followed, laughing.

"What type of new furniture?"

"A new bed, I don't know who you've had in there," I said over my shoulder.

He laughed some more. "Trust me, baby, you're the only woman I've had here."

I wasn't sure I believed him but I smiled anyway.

The front door to his apartment was open and I walked in. I stood and looked around. I loved the apartment and it would certainly do us well to start with.

"I want to put my momma's money to good use. She believed in me, and my passion for designing clothes. I want to open a clothing store, Mack. I want to feature new designers and help them get started. Will you help me with that?"

"I'll do anything you want me to do. When do we start?"

"As soon as I've sold the house. You said I owned it, so what do I do?"

"I can organize that, if that's what you really want to do. Do you want to return there, sort some things?"

"No. I've thought about it. That's not my life anymore, and I don't want anything from it. My life is with you, and Joe and Evelyn, even Miserable Man whose name I know as Paulo, or Paul, or whatever."

"Miserable Man?" Mack laughed. "Yeah, he's not always the friendliest."

"I'm going to be nineteen in a couple of weeks. I want to be married before I'm twenty, that okay with you?" I said, smirking at him and raising my eyebrows in challenge.

"Ma'am, that's most certainly okay with me. But, before you start to clear out my apartment, I want to fuck you in every room."

He stalked toward me, backing me up to the couch. My legs hit it and I fell, he gently fell on top.

"I guess we start here," he said.

———

Later that evening Joe visited. I think he was pretty pissed that I hadn't returned home. He was shadowed by Evelyn, who pulled on his arm to slow down the pace at which he strode around the living room. He gesticulated with his arms widely; he spoke only in Italian, turning to both of us as if he expected we'd understand what he was so stressed about. Evelyn bit her lip, I assumed to stop herself from speaking, or laughing. The creases around her eyes suggested she wasn't taking her father as seriously as I was. The man terrified me at that moment.

Mack was defiant; he placed his arm around my shoulder. On occasion, he opened his mouth to speak but quickly closed it. I could see the smirk forming the more Joe paced and gestured. After a minute or two, Evelyn stepped forward. She placed a hand on her father's arm. He stopped to look at her.

"Papa, I'm going to say one word to you…Rocco."

The room stilled, settled. It was instant. Whatever that word meant to them all, it had the desired effect. Joe relaxed; in fact I swear he shrunk an inch or two. He turned to me.

"Is this what you want? To live with him before you marry?" he asked.

So that was what all the pacing, gesticulating, and raised voices were about?

I nodded. "Joe, I'm nearly nineteen, whether I'm as much of a grown woman as you think I should be before making this decision, I've made it. Mack is it for me, I know in here." I placed my hand over my heart.

Joe simply nodded. He then turned to Mack and poked him in the chest; he reverted back to Italian.

"Yes," Mack said.

Joe nodded and then, without a word, walked out of the apartment. Evelyn rushed after him, but before she disappeared from the room, she looked over her shoulder.

"I'll be back later," she said with a smile.

I don't think either of us spoke for a good minute or two. Eventually, I turned to Mack.

"What on earth was that all about?"

Mack shrugged his shoulders. "I have no idea, I don't understand him when he speaks so fast."

"But you said, 'yes.'"

"And the fact he nodded and walked away, I guess it was the right answer."

I laughed, Mack laughed and pulled me closer into his side.

"Well, here we are. What do you want to do?" he said, looking down at me.

I did nothing but raise my eyebrows at him, perhaps I ran my tongue over my lower lip a little. Mack picked me up and walked us to the bedroom. He kicked the door shut behind him.

Maybe Evelyn did return, I wasn't sure. We didn't leave the bed for the rest of the evening. It was in the early hours of the morning when Mack was sleeping that I rose, thirsty. I walked to the kitchen and turned on the faucet, letting the water run for a little while before I placed a glass underneath.

I stood and looked out the window, over the roofs and the tops of trees that lined the street. I smiled and shook my head.

Never, in all my short life, would I have imagined the past few months. I'd been caught up in a whirlwind and I had no desire to get out.

Letter from Taylor

I never left Mack's apartment and I had loads of fun arguing with him on what needed to go and what got to stay. I didn't want to wipe out his old life completely, but I wanted him, and me, to have a fresh start. Evelyn helped, and I think the poor guy felt bullied to the point he held up his hands and retreated.

My life started that day. I had a man who loved me fiercely, and a family that would become my own. I had money in the bank and a project to start working on. Joe not only owned residential property, he also owned commercial property. He found a perfect one for me in a location he assured me was up and coming. I trusted his judgment, and although I didn't open that store for a while, it was good to know I owned it. When I was ready, I was going into business for myself.

I married Mack with just our family surrounding us. I didn't want extravagance, just him, and the people I'd come to care so much about. It was a wonderful day, made all the better by the surprise appearance of Carol. Mack had tracked her down. She hadn't known that I'd never return, she'd cried for me, so she said. She'd left my father's employment the day he'd sent me away, and she'd spent every day since thinking of me. I told her that I'd tried to call and she was furious that her godson had never passed on the message. She hugged me and shed tears that my mother had not been able to witness me marrying a man I was so deeply in love with.

Life with the Morietti family isn't something I dreamed of, something that I planned for. In truth, I guessed I'd marry the son of a business associate of my father's, a nice 'Harvard type.' Boy, am I glad I didn't!

Mack is fierce and bossy; we clash because we are both strong, and we love so hard. He is my world, as I am his.

Thank you for reading my story, although this was just the beginning of a long and very exciting life as Mack's wife.

Taylor

Taylor and Mack are characters within the Fallen Angel Series. The series is complete and can be found on all major retailers, start your journey with Fallen Angel, Part 1 and meet Brooke and Robert, Evelyn, Travis, and, of course, all those wonderful people that make up a mafia family in Washington, D.C.

If you'd like to read more, start the Fallen Angel journey with Fallen Angel, Part 1, which is free on all retailers...

http://mybook.to/FallenAngelPart1

books2read.com/u/3n1vBb

ABOUT THE AUTHOR

Tracie Podger currently lives in Kent, UK with her husband and a rather obnoxious cat called George. She's a Padi Scuba Diving Instructor with a passion for writing. Tracie has been fortunate to have dived some of the wonderful oceans of the world where she can indulge in another hobby, underwater photography. She likes getting up close and personal with sharks.

Tracie likes to write in different genres. Her Fallen Angel series and its accompanying books are mafia romance and full of suspense. A Virtual Affair & Letters to Lincoln are contemporary romance/women's fiction, and Gabriel, A Deadly Sin & Harlot are thriller/suspense. The Facilitator is erotic romance.

AVAILABLE FROM ALL RETAILERS

Fallen Angel, Part 1

Fallen Angel, Part 2

Fallen Angel, Part 3

Fallen Angel, Part 4

The Fallen Angel Box Set

Evelyn - A Novella – To accompany the Fallen Angel Series

Rocco – A Novella – To accompany the Fallen Angel Series

Robert – To accompany the Fallen Angel Series

Travis – To accompany the Fallen Angel Series

A Virtual Affair – A standalone and available in KindleUnlimited

Gabriel – A standalone and available in KindleUnlimited

The Facilitator – A standalone and available in KindleUnlimited

A Deadly Sin – A standalone and available in KindleUnlimited

Harlot – A standalone and available in KindleUnlimited

Letters to Lincoln – A standalone

Jackson – A Standalone

COMING SOON

Allana – thriller/suspense

A Deadly Mission – thriller/suspense

Stalker Links

https://www.facebook.com/TraciePodgerAuthor/

http://www.TraciePodger.com

Don't forget, if you'd like a free copy of my novella, Evelyn, you've met her now, sign to my mailing list – you'll find the details on my website under 'Newsletter'.

Fallen Angel, Part 1 – A sneak preview

It was in a small room in an office block in Washington, DC, that my life changed, forever.

Sam, my best friend, was sitting at his desk, occupied by a call. Whilst waiting, I headed to the kitchen; some coffee was needed to get me over the jet lag I was feeling.

It was the oddest thing; I simply felt someone behind me, and my heart quickened in fear. There had been no sound, no footsteps, or the noise of the door opening. My hands gripped the counter before I slowly turned around. I found myself looking into the darkest eyes I had ever seen, the blackness took my breath away. It took all my strength to draw my eyes away to look at his face and then he smiled, unblinking at me. He was so close, I could feel his breath, and I couldn't move, I couldn't breathe.

He was tall, over six feet and powerfully built. His shoulders were well-defined in his suit. His black hair was cropped short at the sides, slightly longer and spiked on top. He had a little stubble around a strong jawline and a slight crook to his nose. If anyone could be described as perfect, it was that man.

I guessed him to be in his thirties with just the right amount of laughter lines around his eyes to soften the intensity of him, slightly. As he looked at me, his eyes seemed to grow darker. I felt a heat creep up my neck and my stomach knotted. The air around me felt charged and sparked with electricity and yet he did not say one word.

"There you are," I heard. "I've been looking for you, are you ready to go?"

I looked over to Sam and found my mouth so dry I couldn't speak, so just nodded. He slowly turned to Sam.

"Oh, good evening, Mr. Stone. I didn't realise you were working late," Sam stammered.

"Always, Sam. Now, introduce me to your friend," he replied, his voice was low and commanding.

"Brooke, this is Mr. Stone, owner of Vassago. Mr. Stone, my friend from England, Brooke Stiles. She arrived this morning, to stay with me."

Mr. Stone turned back to me, a slow smile crept across his face, and he held his hand out. I took it and as his hand closed around mine, images flooded my brain, too fast to be able to see any one of them, but it unnerved me greatly.

"Pleased to meet you, Miss Stiles. I look forward to seeing more of you," he said, as his dark eyes bored straight through me.

"Umm, pleased to meet you too, Mr. Stone," I replied.

With that, he let go of my hand, nodded to Sam, and walked away. Finally, I let out the breath I was holding and felt my legs start to shake. Glancing up at Sam, he was smiling with a quizzical look on his face.

"Wow, what just happened there?" Sam asked.

"Oh my God, Sam, I don't know. I came to make some coffee and just felt someone behind me, I turned and there he was, just staring at me," I replied.

"Come on, honey, let's go searching. I'm starving and you can tell me all about it."

Ever since I could remember, I've felt like I was searching for something. There was something missing from my life, a piece of a jigsaw to fit before I was complete. I'd tried to explain it to Sam many times, but I had no idea what it was I was looking for. It became our joke, instead of saying *let's go out,* it was *let's go searching.*

We linked arms and left the building, Sam led the way. We planned to meet his boyfriend, Scott, for a meal before jet lag finally took hold of me. The restaurant was lovely, the food good, but I felt so unsettled. I couldn't place what was wrong with me and putting it down to the journey, I tried to enjoy my evening with my two favourite guys.

I had missed Sam so much, we'd been best friends since we were five years old. I remembered that I'd cried and clung to him at the airport when he'd left the UK. Thank God for email and Facebook, a cheap way to keep in contact. It had been wonderful to hear about Sam settle into the Washington life and to see his relationship with Scott bloom. More importantly, it was great to see his career take off at Vassago Corp, one of the largest property development companies in the USA.

Sam told Scott that we had bumped into Mr. Stone in the kitchen and Scott wanted the details. It seemed Mr. Stone was a bit of an enigma, closeted away in his penthouse office. He would be seen wandering around occasionally and the most people would receive would be a nod and maybe a smile.

"Oh, Scott, it was so strange. One minute I was there on my own making coffee and next, I just felt him behind me. The hair on my arms stood to attention. I didn't hear him come into the room at all. But bloody hell, Scott, looking in his eyes is like staring straight at the devil himself," I told him.

The memory provoked a shiver. "I've never felt anything so intense in all my life."

"Honey, pray, tell us more?" Sam asked, dramatically.

"Well, I don't know how to explain it. It was like he just absorbed me, he didn't speak words but his eyes spoke volumes," I said.

We finished our meal and stifling a yawn, we made the short walk back to the apartment. The guys lived in Columbia Heights, not far from the Tivoli Theatre, a wonderful, diverse area of DC. It was full of restaurants and colourful bars. After walking out of a ten-year relationship back home, Sam, and a holiday in America, was just what I needed.

That night I dreamed of Mr. Stone, or to be more precise, I dreamed of his eyes, how dangerous and alluring they were at the same time. What puzzled me was that I wanted to see him again. The thing that disturbed me, the thing I had not told Sam or Scott was the feeling of familiarity I felt. I knew that man yet I'd never met him before. Something deep inside me confirmed what I felt —I really did know that man.

<hr />

I woke late the following morning, my body clock still adjusting to the time difference, and stiff from sleeping in a strange bed. Sam had already left for work. I knew that he hadn't been able to get much time off during my visit, but I didn't mind. I enjoyed my own company and it would give me time to think about my situation back home. It was only a couple of weeks prior that I'd ended the relationship with Michael and needed to get my head together. Being with my best friend as well as having some time on my own, would help me do that. More so, what I needed was a gym. Pounding away on the treadmill was my way of getting rid of all the stress that had been building for the past couple of years. I sent a text to Sam asking if there was a local gym I could use.

Sam called me straight back.

"Honey, there's a gym in the basement of my office, I'll call reception and get you a pass. Maybe I'll meet you."

It sounded like a good plan to me, so I packed my gym kit and made my way to his office. I signed in with security and was given a pass and instructions of where to go.

I knew Sam was on the tenth floor and there appeared to be at least another three above that. Having to stop once to ask for directions, I eventually found the changing rooms and put on my workout gear. A mile run would clear my stuffy head and loosen my limbs. I liked to keep fit and the solitude of running alone gave me time to think.

I entered the gym. Sam hadn't arrived and focusing on the treadmills, without catching anyone's eye, I made my way over. There were a couple of people already there, getting a lunchtime workout. I plugged in my iPod and started with a gentle jog, increasing the speed until I was at a comfortable run. The treadmills faced a wall of mirrors, something I normally hated. I didn't like to look at myself sweaty and panting.

However, looking in those mirrors I was able to scan the room. There was a range of high tech equipment, running, rowing, and weights, and in the far corner a boxing ring. Surrounding it were punch bags and speedballs. Kickboxing was something I had learned to do so I watched as a couple of guys warmed up, ready for a workout. I noticed him straight away of course. Although his back was facing me, I knew it was him. Stone, in shorts and a vest top, his hands bandaged, and his hair already slick with sweat. His bulging arms glistened and his vest had stuck to his back. I stumbled a little, losing my step and slowed down the treadmill. I'd taken a machine in the far corner in the hope of not being noticed by anyone and was glad of that.

I watched as he pounded the punch bag, he obviously knew what he was doing. He looked every much the professional boxer. He skipped around while his friend held the bag steady, only just though. He hit the bag with such force his friend would stumble a little having to correct himself quickly as another succession of punches found its target. They carried that on for a little while and then I watched him stop and raise his vest to wipe the sweat from his eyes.

He had the most amazing body. His stomach was taut, muscular, and when he turned around his whole back was covered in one large tattoo. It looked like an angel, a body with wings. I glanced around; I noticed several other women and saw that all eyes were on him.

I tried to concentrate on my run, closing my eyes briefly so as to not be distracted by the image of him. I was out of luck; he was imprinted behind my eyelids. Hearing him laugh, a low throaty noise, I watched as he climbed into the ring. A third, older man, laced their gloves and the two friends boxed, pounding away, and making me wince.

They laughed, taunted each other and I found that I couldn't take my eyes off them. Luckily at no time had he looked my way, so focused on what he was doing and I managed to get through my run. The machine beeped telling me that my mile was up and it started to slow, to warm down, and come to a stop. I leaned forward on the rails and steadied my breathing. I doubted my rapid heartbeat was just because of my run, I suspected it was also the effect of watching Stone.

"Miss Stiles?" I heard.

I turned to see him standing next to the machine, again he had managed to sneak up on me without a sound, making me start. I looked around and noticed the other women watching me, wondering who I was, I guessed, and why did I get his attention and not them. It was obvious they were not here to workout; their perfectly made up faces and not a bead of sweat on their brows gave them away. Taking my towel, I wiped it across my face conscious that I looked hot and sweaty. I watched a bead of sweat roll from his forehead, cross his temple and I wanted to reach out, trap it with my finger, and taste it. I blinked, rapidly, shocked at the thought.

"Hello again, Mr. Stone. I was waiting for Sam but I guess he worked through lunch," I blurted out.

Why did that man make me feel so uncomfortable?

"Do you work out here often?" I added, and then realised that was a stupid thing to say.

His eyebrows shot up and a smirk played on his lips. "Everyday," he replied.

I fidgeted, eager to leave. I wanted to get away from that stare.

"Um, well, I guess I ought to take a shower, nice to meet you again," I said and scurried away.

Without looking, I knew he was watching me leave.

I stood under the shower lost in my thoughts. "How do I know you?" I whispered.

Once I'd dressed I found my phone and noticed a text from Sam, he would have to work through lunch. He was sorry, an unexpected meeting came up, but he would catch up with me later. I decided to take a walk and leaving my gym bag behind in a locker, I headed off to see some of the sights of Washington.

I was having a lovely time, that was until the black Range Rover pulled alongside me. It had blacked out windows, chrome finishes, and I had no idea of its occupants. I was standing on the pavement wanting to take a photograph when the car had pulled over. The rear door opened and I stepped back, assuming its occupants wanted to exit and to be honest, was a bit annoyed they had to choose that exact spot.

I moved slightly away and raised my camera. As I concentrated on the picture I wanted to take, I felt the air around me change; it became dense. Looking to one side, he was there. Stone had exited the car so silently and was standing beside me.

"Brooke, can you get in the car?" he asked, his hand held the door open.

I looked at him, stunned. "Excuse me?" I replied, shocked at his request.

"Can you get in the car, *please*? I would like to take you to lunch."

Lunch? What planet was that man on? How on earth did he know

I was there? I wouldn't flatter myself to think he was following me but I didn't believe in coincidence. I stood my ground, though he still unnerved me.

"Thank you for the invitation, but I'm sure you have better things to do. I'm sorry, Mr. Stone, but I've already eaten."

I watched a slow smile cross his face and those eyes bore into me. I was rooted to the spot. I got the feeling that Stone was a man not turned down very often. He did, thankfully, seem a little amused by it.

"No you haven't, but that's okay, you don't want lunch so instead we'll have dinner."

Before I could even reply, he turned, got back into the car and it moved away. In all my thirty years I don't think anyone had spoken to me that way, demanded my time and attention and made me feel so totally confused. I needed to speak to Sam but he was busy, so I left a message for him to call me back when he could. My tour of the city didn't seem so appealing anymore.

Fuck you, Mr. Stone, I thought.

He had seriously spoiled my day but somehow I knew I would go to dinner. He intrigued me and I racked my brain to remember how I knew him. As I made my way home, Sam returned my call.

"Hey honey, I've just received a call from Mr. Stone himself, can you believe that? He asked me if we had plans as he wants to take you to dinner tonight."

"Jesus, Sam. I went to the gym and he was there, boxing. It was just so embarrassing. He came over, and I'm standing there all red-faced and sweaty. Next thing, I'm on the street, taking a photo and a Range Rover pulls up alongside me. He demands I get in the car, he's taking me to lunch."

"What did you say?"

"I told him I'd already eaten. I've met the man for a couple of minutes and now he wants to take me to lunch." I then recount the rest of the story about the dinner invitation.

"What's up with this man, Sam? There's something really strange about him."

"You know what, I've only met him a couple of times and I've been here three years. No one really knows that much about him. I mean, he's often in the society pages but other than that, I don't know. Exciting though, isn't it?" he said.

I wasn't sure 'exciting' was the word I would have chosen. He was very compelling, and attractive of course, but there were undercurrents of such power it was scary. I was reminded of a film, I couldn't remember the name. Al Pacino played a powerful businessman who turned out to be the devil himself. When I'd arrived back at Sam's I opened the door and noticed an envelope on the floor. It was hand written, addressed to me, I opened it and took out a small white card.

Brooke, Dinner, Seven o'clock, I'll send a car. Robert Stone

I flopped on the sofa; I needed a beer. So his name was Robert.

Somehow I didn't see him as a Robert; perhaps Damien would have been more appropriate. I wondered if I would just ignore the knock on the door when 'the car' arrived. I would go though, because something in the back of my mind niggled at me; a feeling of familiarity. Without realising, I spent an awful amount of time getting ready; making sure my black hair shone and my makeup was perfect. I'd selected a fitted red dress to wear, something bold to give me the confidence I needed.

At exactly seven o'clock I heard a buzz on the intercom. I walked down to the main door and opened it to find a man, not Stone, in a grey suit. The black Range Rover was at the curb. It was the same man I'd seen him spar with earlier. He was as muscular, but with blond, short hair and blue eyes—the total opposite of Stone.

"Miss Stiles, would you like me to take your coat?" he said, as he escorted me to the car.

"Thank you, but I can carry it," I replied.

I felt agitated, more at myself for accepting the dinner invitation. As much as I wanted to go, I also didn't. It was so confusing.

I couldn't place his accent. Although it was American, I thought there was a slight Irish twang to it. He opened the rear door and not another word was spoken until we pulled outside a brick building with just a gloss black door and a gold handle. It didn't look like a restaurant and I hoped to God it wasn't his house. I sat until the car door was opened for me and before I took the last step up to the gloss door, it was also opened.

"Miss Stiles, please follow me," said yet another suited, rather formal looking guy.

Inside, the building was obviously some kind of exclusive restaurant. Rich, brown coloured walls, matching leather chairs around tables with crisp white linen and silver cutlery adorned the vast room. I was led to an alcove, an area slightly away from the main seating and screened off by planting.

It was a truly wonderful place and obviously very expensive. As I approached, he stood. Those black eyes stared straight at me. He nodded to the concierge and pulled the chair out. Using his hand on my back, he guided me to my seat. I wanted to recoil at his touch, not that it was horrible but I could feel a searing heat where his hand had been and a tingling all over my flesh. It unsettled me. He gestured to a glass, already filled with red wine. I took a large sip to steady my nerves.

"I'm glad you came, Brooke," he said.

"I'm not sure you gave me much choice, Mr. Stone," I replied.

He laughed a little, "Please, call me Robert."

"Well then, Robert, thank you for the invitation. This is an amazing place," I said, looking around. He simply smiled.

"I've taken the liberty of ordering for you, I trust you don't mind," he told me.

To be honest, yes I did mind, but I didn't want to offend any more than I had to so I smiled my thanks.

"You seem nervous," he said.

I tried to hold his gaze, "Well, I, um," I stumbled.

I couldn't find the words to explain I'd never done that before, met someone for a couple of minutes and then agreed to dinner.

"Tell me about yourself," he said, cutting short my answer.

I was a little unsure what to say. How much does one divulge to a complete stranger, one that not only intrigued, but also unsettled me.

"Well, I live in the UK, obviously, in Kent. I'm here on holiday, and like Sam, I work in marketing but for an agency in London. Sam and I have been friends since we were little and I haven't seen him for a while so thought I would come and visit."

I didn't want to go into too much detail about why I was there; I tried to keep the conversation light.

"So where are you really from? Your black hair, blue eyes and fair skin, that's not typically British," he asked, leaning slightly towards me.

"I don't know." I answered, uncomfortable with his scrutinising of me.

"Perhaps there's a little Irish on my father's side. I must admit, I look nothing like my parents," I added with a nervous chuckle.

The whole time I'd spoken he'd looked at me. Even when our starter was laid in front of us, he picked up his fork and ate without taking his eyes from mine. I found at first it was too hard to look back at him, to hold his stare, but the more I spoke, the more I found I couldn't look anywhere else.

It was as if there *was* nothing else, just the table and Robert Stone. I don't believe I could even hear anything around me. I didn't notice the waiter remove my plate, replace it with another, or replenish my glass. It was as if time did not exist, just the moment.

Before I'd realised, we had finished our meal. I can't tell you what I ate but I know that I'd not stopped talking and he had hardly said a word. How had he managed to get me to do that? Being a reserved person, I didn't share what was in my head, yet I'd told a stranger my life story. It was as if his stillness, his quietness, drew the words from me.

I seemed to run out of things to say and the air stilled around me. It was suffocating and I had an urge to leave. Perhaps he saw my discomfort because he folded his napkin and placed it on the table.

"Would you like to leave?" he asked, I nodded.

He held out his hand and led me from the restaurant. It hadn't dawned on me that there had been no bill, we'd simply walked straight out to the waiting car. For the second time, I slid across the black leather seats and Robert spoke quietly to the driver.

"I would like to show you something, if you're not in a rush to return home," he said as he joined me.

We drove the short distance to the office where Sam worked, the building Robert owned. We exited the car and walked into the foyer, past the security guards who seemed to stand to attention. With his hand on my back, Robert guided me into the lift. Again, I felt that heat where his hand touched and a tingle across my skin. I noticed a small keypad and watched as his fingers keyed in a code and the lift ascended, beyond the floors that were numbered.

The doors slid open into a reception so very different to the rest of the building. The floor was a dark oak, a glass, abstract sculpture stood in the middle of the area and beyond was a single, large door. Taking a key, he opened it and we entered a penthouse apartment. I was not ready for that. I had no idea I would be taken back to the place I assumed he lived in, but I was totally blown away; the apartment was stunning.

The walls were a stark white, a large black leather sofa dominated the lounge area, and a sound system hung on the wall. Walking to it, he pressed a button and music flowed through the whole apartment.

One wall was completely glass, slightly tinted and I walked across and looked out. The view was breathtaking. Washington was spread out below me. The lights of the buildings, the traffic, the White House in the distance, all shone in the night. I could see for miles.

Robert moved behind me, again so silently it took me by surprise to see his reflection in the glass. I felt like his prey and my nerves were on alert. My heart hammered in my chest and my breath caught in my throat. He stood directly behind me; I felt an immense heat radiating from him and a strange, magnetic pull towards him. It was as if my muscles took on a will of their own and my body needed to be close to his.

"Thank you for spending your evening with me," he whispered, his breath caressed the side of my neck.

"Do you like the view? This is what I wanted to show you," he added.

He described some of the landmarks, leaning so close with his arm pointing over my shoulder. All the time I looked at his reflection, at his mouth. I wanted to taste him, to feel his lips on mine and it troubled me to feel, to think that way.

"It's wonderful, do you live here?" I asked, forcing my eyes away from his and back to the view.

"Not permanently. I have a house outside the city in Great Falls. Perhaps you would like to visit."

"Can I ask you something?" I asked.

"Sure."

"Why did you invite me to dinner? I mean, you only met me for a couple of minutes really. It's a bit odd, don't you think?"

"Not odd enough for you to refuse," he replied unsmiling. "I met you, I wanted to know more about you."

We fell silent looking at the view below. He lifted his hand and moved some hair from my shoulder exposing my neck. He lowered his head and placed a small kiss on the side, his eyes met mine in the reflection of the glass; there was a question in them.

I should have been outraged but I wasn't, I just felt an immediate attraction to him. A fire raged in the pit of my stomach, my heart missed a beat, fluttering in my chest and I felt my legs start to shake. I wanted to lean back into him, to feel his body against mine. All the time I faced the glass wall with him behind me, watching his reflection.

"I want you, Brooke," he softly said.

I couldn't answer; I felt entranced and all rational thought left my brain leaving nothing but an overwhelming desire for him. I gently nodded my head.

He unzipped my dress and it fell, crumpled around my feet leaving me standing in just my underwear and shoes. I stepped out of the dress, I wanted to turn and face him, but he held my hips, keeping me still. With one hand he ran his fingers up my spine sending shivers through my body. His hands travelled over my shoulders and down my arms, holding them to my waist while his lips trailed a path from my neck to my ear. I wanted to reach up, to run my hand through his hair, to touch him, but all the time he held me still.

A small moan escaped my lips and I felt him smile at my response. A burn started between my legs, my body was aching with desire for him. One arm circled my waist and with the other he ran his fingers down my throat, over the top of my breasts and down my stomach.

"Do you know what I want to do, Brooke? I want to watch you come and then I want to fuck you."

Although the words were harsh they were said with a strange softness. His hand moved to mine, covering it and he ran both to the top of my panties. He slid our fingers under the material. All the time, his head was just above my shoulder, looking at me in the glass.

I held his gaze and swallowed hard. I licked my lips in anticipation of what was to come. Our fingers brushed across my clitoris, gently teasing, his fingers circling and squeezing as they guided mine. I gasped, the throbbing escalated with every movement he made. My legs shook and I leaned back into him for support. His other hand cupped my breast, rubbing across the nipple.

He pushed my hand further down, using his finger to push mine inside me. I was so hot, so wet. It was erotic, both of us inside me at the same time and I cried out. Our fingers were slickly entwined. He took my hand, trailing our fingers over my body and raised them to my mouth. He ran my finger over my lips.

"Suck," he whispered.

I opened my lips slightly allowing him to push my finger into my mouth and I tasted that sweet, metallic taste of me. His eyes never left mine and no matter whether I wanted to or not, I could not look away, I could not close mine. I was totally devoured by him.

Robert grabbed my shoulders and turned me so quickly I nearly lost my balance. His lips were hard on mine; his tongue forced its way into my mouth. His hands gripped the sides of my face and he held me to him. I raised my hands to his head, running my fingers through his hair.

I could feel his erection pushing into my stomach and I wanted him as much as he clearly wanted me. As he stepped back his teeth pulled on my lower lip sending a delectable pain shooting through me.

He looked down at me and smiled. He took my hand and led me to his bedroom. I reached down to remove a shoe.

"Leave them on," he said.

We walked across the lounge and he opened a door into his bedroom. The only furniture was a bed that occupied the center of the room with two small tables either side. There was a glass wall on one side of the room and two doors on the other. I turned to face him and reaching up to undo the buttons, I slowly slid his shirt from his shoulders and let it fall to the floor. I ran my hands over his chest; he was so well-defined, sculpted even, with a faint scar running down his side.

My fingers ran down his stomach to the top of his jeans. I undid his belt, pulling it from the loops, then the button, and the zip.

Allowing them to slide down, he kicked off his shoes. Stepping back I was able to look at him.

As much as he intimidated me, I wanted to take him all in, every curve of his body, every hair and commit it to memory. Yet as I did, I realised, I already knew it. I kissed his chest, gently bit his nipples, and let my tongue travel over his stomach. His hands wrapped in my hair, guiding me.

My fingers, either side of his very tight shorts, hooked under and I pulled them down. His erection sprang free and my hand caressed him, feeling the silkiness of his skin as my nails scraped gently against him.

I listened to his breathing change, become rapid, raspier, and it pleased me to hear the effect I had on him. He pulled my face towards him, his mouth found mine and he kissed me hard. He undid my bra, letting it fall from my shoulders and his mouth travelled over my breasts to the nipples. He sucked and bit one then the other, marking my skin.

My hands were in his short hair, my fingers dug into his skull as the most intense feelings of desire flooded through me. Feelings far stronger than any I'd felt before. Just his hands on my body were enough to make my legs shake and my stomach flip.

He walked me backwards towards the bed and then picked me up. Putting me gently down with my head resting on the pillows, he moved to the end and climbed on. Removing one shoe, he brought my foot to his lips kissing the arch, my ankle, and all the way up the inside of my leg, stopping at the top of my thigh. His mouth travelled down my other leg, removing the shoe and his teeth nipped my toes.

Moving up and over me, he hooked his fingers in my panties and pulled them down. His mouth was on my stomach; his tongue probed my navel, sliding down until it circled my clitoris. My hands gripped the bedding as his tongue flicked in and out of me while he gripped my hips, holding me still.

I wanted to arch my back, to force his tongue further inside me. He brought me to the brink of an orgasm and then he bit me. While I was coming, the most exquisite pain shot through me, intensifying the feeling; every nerve ending burned and I screamed out.

He moved above me, his legs forced mine further apart and he reached over to the table. He ripped open a foil packet with his teeth and without taking his eyes from mine he placed a condom on himself. Supporting himself on his arms, his hands held mine above my head. The tip of his cock just brushed against me. I wanted him in me so I raised my hips. Every time I did, he moved just out of reach. All the time his dark eyes bore into me, straight to my soul.

"Do you want me to fuck you, Brooke?" he whispered.

Oh God, did I! "Yes," I said as he gently rubbed against me, tormenting me.

"Look at me," he demanded as he slammed into me.

He completely filled me and I cried out. He stilled before moving again, so slowly yet so deeply inside me. He was totally in control of my body, and my mind. He decided when to bring me to the brink of an orgasm and then stop. It was terrible and wonderful at the same time. I wanted to just let go but he wouldn't let me. I was totally at his mercy and I loved it.

He moved in and out of me, picking up the pace until neither of us could hold on anymore. His mouth crashed onto mine and our teeth clashed, his tongue forced its way in as we came. For the first time in the whole evening I watched him lose control, unravel a little. It was only for a spit second but I'd seen it. He released my hands and rested his forehead on mine as he tried to slow his breathing with his eyes closed. I felt his heartbeat race and I wrapped my arms around him, holding him to me. It was a moment of vulnerability that I got the immediate impression he did not show often.

He rolled off me, pulled me onto my side and facing each other, we lay for a while. He removed the condom and then wrapping one arm around me, he stroked the side of my face. It was a tender moment and when I looked into his eyes I got a fleeting glimpse of a lost soul.

"Thank you," he whispered. "Will you stay the night?"

I closed my eyes for a moment and then reality hit. What on earth had I just done? Having sex with someone on a first date, staying the night was not something I did, normally. There was a slight wretched tone to his voice when he'd asked and I knew for some reason, at that moment, he needed me.

He was intense, closed, and somehow I knew, trouble. But I wanted to comfort him, to have him fall asleep in my arms. It just felt the right thing to do.

"I need to text Sam," I told him as I moved out of the bed.

I felt no awkwardness walking naked to where I'd left my bag. I felt no embarrassment in him watching me as I sent a text, telling Sam I was fine and that I would see him in the morning. Turning the phone off, I returned to the bedroom, climbed back in the bed and snuggled into his arms.

"Robert, I've just had great sex with you," I smiled. "I don't know anything about you though. I don't do this normally; I don't sleep around. I have no idea what just happened there, I want you to know that," I said.

"I know. So what do you want to know?" he replied.

"Well, tell me something about yourself."

"I was born in London, my parents died when I was six or seven and I was sent to America to live with an old, mad, religious aunt I'd never met before," he said.

"I spent time running away, living rough, getting in with the wrong people and doing very bad things, but I made a great deal of money along the way," he continued.

I was stunned, but more importantly, he seemed shocked that he'd just told me that. I didn't want to hear about the bad things but I felt terribly sorry for him. It must have been awful to have lost his parents, move countries, and live with someone he didn't know. Despite knowing he might be trouble, I wanted to know more. Something pulled at my heart, especially when I watched him drift into sleep. Peacefulness settled over his face and I truly believed the person I was looking at then was not the person many people got to see.

Despite never having done that before, I was glad for that night, glad that I was there when he needed me. I was glad that he'd shared a piece of himself that I guessed was normally hidden, and with a smile on my face, I acknowledged, the sex was the best I'd ever had.

You can read the rest of Fallen Angel, Part 1 for free – available on all retailers.

Printed in Great Britain
by Amazon